BLOOD TRACKS

Kevin O'Hagan

Grosvenor House
Publishing Limited

Cover design by Tom O'Hagan

This book is published by
Grosvenor House Publishing Ltd
Link House
140 The Broadway, Tolworth, Surrey, KT6 7HT.
www.grosvenorhousepublishing.co.uk

A CIP record for this book
is available from the British Library

ISBN 978-1-80381-079-9

Previous novels by the author

Battlescars
No Hiding Place
Last Stand
Killing Time
A Change of Heart

'There's a killer on the loose again
Standing in the shadows
A killer on the loose
There's a killer on the loose again
Coming to get you.'

Thin Lizzy, 'Killer on the Loose', 1980

Author's Note

Some cities, towns and locations and people mentioned in this novel exist in real life. The island of Ruma is completely fictional, as are its landmarks in the story. Landscapes and layouts take on another imaginary life in this book. All the characters are purely fictional as are their stories. Thank you for indulging me to help in creating this book.

Dedication

To all my friends, family and the millions
across the world who have been affected by COVID.

May we all see better times ahead for all.

God bless.

Preface

Well, here we are again, dear reader. A new novel has been written. This latest effort was an absolute pleasure to write as it centred around one of my lifelong passions – music. I decided to combine it with a splash of horror and a big dollop of suspense and intrigue. So here we have *Blood Tracks*.

The story takes on a well-worn path of book and film about a group of guests stranded in a spooky old building, but this version has a modern gritty twist that you will hopefully find fresh, exciting and suspenseful.

Also, it will keep you guessing right up to the final pages.

As always, any project you embark on, you will need a little help. Big thanks to my daughter, Lauren, for her proofreading and to my son, Tom, for the cover design.

I wrote most of this book waiting to move into a new house, which became a nightmare and I am extremely grateful to my son, Jake, and his wife, Soeli, for letting my wife, Tina, and I stay at their house. Sorry it turned out longer than planned. Love to you both for your generosity and kindness.

As always, big love and thanks to my wife, Tina, for being my rock and supporting all I do. I am a very lucky man.

Thank you to my publishers, Grosvenor House Publishing, for their excellent support and professional advice.

Finally, massive thanks to you, the reader, for supporting my writing and buying this book.

I hope you enjoy it as much as I enjoyed writing it.

Thank you.

Kevin O'Hagan, 2022

Chapter 1

1984. Castle Donington Park, Derbyshire. The Monsters of Rock festival.

Jimmy Parish, the lead singer of the hugely successful rock band, Stormtrooper, looked out into the huge sea of faces in the crowd. They stretched way back beyond his vision. Bobbing heads, swaying bodies and hands raised aloft. Each and every one of them lost in the sweet moment that only music can bring to your heart and mind.

An audience of 70,000 people were crammed into the venue. Parish had them eating out the palm of his hand as the band were concluding their blistering encore with one of their biggest hits to date, "Tough Love". They had just performed a storming set to headline the Monsters of Rock festival and it couldn't have gone better.

In previous years they had been way down the line-up as they strived to emulate their peers who had graced the main stage. Giants of rock, such as Rainbow, Dio, Saxon, Judas Priest and Whitesnake. In the last couple of years, Stormtrooper had a meteoric rise to be the top dogs of their trade. They were riding high on a crazy wave of mega rock stardom. Closing the iconic festival on a perfect August summer night was the icing on the cake to their most successful year yet. They had headlined this evening above the likes of Mötley Crüe, Gary Moore and Van Halen. No mean feat.

Their fourth album, *Riding Shotgun,* had just hit number one in the UK and the States. The first single off the album, entitled "Burning Ambition", had also just reached the top both sides of the Atlantic. They were hot property and everybody wanted a piece of them. The band had just finished a phenomenal 35-date tour of the USA and had come back to home soil to headline the annual festival. They were determined to make rock history and blow all the other bands out of the water. This was their time and they knew it.

The music business is a fickle one. You can be flavour of the month one minute and then a short while later you can find your music in the bargain basket in Asda next to all the other has-beens. Music longevity came from real artists who could play, sing and write their own music, not some plastic, manufactured, bubblegum with no substance or heart. In this tough and competitive business, you had to know when to seize your moment and Stormtrooper presently were doing that with both hands.

Parish now had the crowd all clapping in time as they repeated the chorus of this huge anthem.

Tough love is all you give me
Tough love is all I get
Tough love is all you give me
But I still want you yet.

This was the perfect moment for any frontman of a band. The power and control was beyond anything you could image. This was the pinnacle of the music world.

Parish, as always on the final song of the encore, threw his trademark jet black tombstone cowboy hat into the crowd. The audience frenziedly scrambled for the precious souvenir worn by their idol.

All was good until Parish froze. He had forgotten his next line. The cocaine he had taken in the break before the encore had kicked in big time. The half a bottle of Jack Daniels drank throughout the show hadn't exactly helped either but it aided Parish to deal with his secret fear – stage fright. He had managed to keep this from the band, disguised behind the bluff and bravado that booze and drugs gave him, but beneath the surface he had been struggling and the cracks had begun to show on their American tour. The drugs he had been taking took him through a gamut of feelings, from euphoria to insecurity to paranoia to anger to fear. He was now experiencing panic as he had dried up and could not think of the lyrics to sing.

Cursing under his breath, lead guitarist, Ricky Wilder, improvised with an electrifying solo. It wasn't the first time on this tour that Jimmy had either forgotten his lines or his cues on stage. He was becoming a fucking liability. The band were riding high on huge success and the lead singer was beginning to lose it.

'Jimmy, get back to the mic and finish it up, for fuck's sake,' shouted Ricky above the noise.

Jimmy looked back at him as if he were a stranger. His dull eyes stared through his bandmate as if he weren't there.

Ricky knew Parish was in trouble. Jimmy Parish's drug and drink problem had jeopardise the band's future more than enough times recently.

Ricky continued playing as he watched Jimmy suddenly launch himself headfirst into the crowd. He was surfed along the adoring hordes until he was finally thrown back on stage. By then, the paramedics were grabbing him and hauling him away. The crowd just thought it was Parish's usual theatrics and took no notice.

Ricky quickly jumped in front of the microphone and sung the conclusion of the song before wrapping up the gig with a farewell bow and a promise to be back soon. The noise of the crowd's applauds was deafening and it really shook the band to its core as they left the stage.

As the band headed backstage, they were greeted with towels and bottled water. Ricky spied their manager, Bernie Garvey. Garvey was in his forties and a by-product of the late 60s and the Woodstock, Hendrix and Rolling Stones era. He had hung around the rock scene since a youngster growing up with the sounds of Elvis, Jerry Lee Lewis, and Chuck Berry.

Bernie had grown up on the Channel Island of Jersey where his father ferried a pleasure boat around the island for tourists and his mother worked at the popular seafront hotel, The Royal Mariner. The hotel always hosted live music and gave new acts to the music scene a debut. Young Bernie loved being able to get a front-row seat to listen to them all and this is where he first dreamt of a career in music. He had watched, amongst many, a fledgling Cliff Richard, Tom Jones and Dusty Springfield perform at the hotel.

Bernie had worked with his father after leaving school but a life on the sea was not for him. He went back to education and finally got a degree in business studies and left the island for London.

With his combined head for business and musical knowledge, he started managing local bands before coming across four lads from Newcastle that were Tyneside's answer to the Rolling Stones, named North Star. They went on to have a dozen or more chart hits in the mid to late sixties and even supported The Beatles, Stones, Animals, and The Troggs.

They were due for big things but tragically three of the band members died in a helicopter accident over the Grand Canyon whilst holidaying in the States when a random flock of birds flew into the rotor blades and the engines failed. It ended the band for good.

In the early 70s, Bernie got in on the glam rock scene and became the manager of Magic Stone, who toured with the mighty Slade, Sweet and T. Rex. Now he was making waves with the heavy metal gods that were Stormtrooper.

His bleached blonde hair couldn't hide his advancing years, and neither could his belly hanging over his trousers but he was a smart cookie with many connections in the dog-eat-dog music business.

'Great set, boys. The crowd fucking loved it. Magical, just magical,' he gushed.

Ricky Wilder wasn't as complimentary. 'What's happened to that prick, Parish?'

'He has gone to hospital as a precaution. Too much coke, I believe. One of the roadies, Eddie, went with him in the ambulance. He will ring me when he knows more. Anyway, don't worry about that. What is it like to be conquering the world, eh?'

Ricky was not to be pacified. 'Never mind all that, when are you going to wake up to the fact Parish is a fucking liability and will ruin this band before it can reach its true potential?' People were now gathering around as they became aware of the heated conversation.

Bernie Garvey was also aware of this fact. 'Look, lads, let's go in here.' He gestured to a private room off stage. He looked at his personal assistant, Joey Ellis. 'Joey, give us 20 minutes. I don't want anybody disturbing us. Do I make myself clear?'

Joey nodded. 'Perfectly, Bernie. You have my word you will not be disturbed.'

Bernie ushered the members of the band into the room and then shut the door behind them. He had a feeling he was not going to like the following conversation. Once inside Bernie ushered the band to chairs that were situated around a large table. Apart from the furniture, the room was empty. Everybody sat except Ricky Wilder.

Bernie spoke. 'Look, Ricky, I understand your concerns. I will speak with Jimmy as soon as he gets out of hospital. I will tell him—'

Bernie was cut off by Wilder. 'Words, Bernie. Fucking words. I have heard it all before. You question Jimmy's behaviour and he soft-soaps you with false promises and you let him off the hook. The band and me have had enough of covering for him. We are on the brink of conquering the world and Parish is a weak link that is going to fuck it all up for us.'

Ray "The hammer" Hawkins, the band's drummer and oldest member, agreed. 'Ricky is right, Bernie. We have dragged his ass out of the shit half a dozen times or more on this tour. He is unpredictable. A fucking loose cannon. Nobody knows what he is going to do next. We can't work like that.'

The rest of the band, which was Rory Doyle (bassist) and Erik Olsen (keyboards), nodded in acknowledgement. This had been one of many incidents on the tour. Parish had been late for rehearsals, sound checks and meetings. He had also forgotten lyrics to songs on one too many nights. Offstage, he had stopped associating with the rest of the band and preferred to hang around with the groupies and hangers-on who milked his ego, played to his vanity and supplied his drugs. Most of the time he was walking around intoxicated or as high as a kite. None of the band were choirboys, but when it came to performing, they were all professional. Jimmy had become the weak link in the chain.

Bernie raised his hands in surrender. 'OK. I hear you but what do you want me to do?'

Wilder looked around at the band and then back to Bernie. 'Sack him. Get rid of him now before it is too late.'

Bernie broke into laughter. 'Sack him. Are you fucking serious? Jimmy Parish is not only the darling lead singer of the band. He is also the main songwriter. Have you all gone mad?'

None of the band shared Bernie Garvey's laughter. 'What the fuck has Jimmy recently written, Bernie? He couldn't even hold a pen at present,' said Ricky.

'He will get back to it soon. We have a number one album and single – you can't do much more than that,' replied Bernie.

'Shit, Bernie, you know as well as I do most of the tracks for the latest album were written over a year ago.

He hasn't lifted a pen to paper since. He is a busted flush.'

Rory Doyle now spoke up. 'Let Ricky take over the lead vocals.'

Bernie's eyes grew wide in disbelief. 'Ricky is the lead guitarist, remember.'

Wilder cut in again. 'I have somebody I know that can walk into this band as lead guitarist. He is a brilliant young American called Marshall Meyers, from Texas. He plays in the band, Wolverine. He has also stepped in and toured with the BOC and Styx. He knows all our stuff. He would be perfect. You know I can sing. I have shared vocals and have sang a few solos. On this latest album I wrote three of the songs. I have more. We can do it. But we need to do it now.'

Bernie Garvey stood up from his chair. 'You seem to have this all worked out by the sounds of it, but you are forgetting one thing – the fans love Jimmy. He is the frontman and has been from day one. It won't work.'

Erik Olsen now took his turn to have his say. 'Not strictly true, Bernie. Look at AC/DC. At the height of their fame, they lost Bon Scott. He was iconic. The band said he was irreplaceable. That they were finished. But they came back six months later with the *Back in Black* album, with Brian Johnson on lead vocals, and they have gone from strength to strength.'

'Then there was Iron Maiden,' added Ricky Wilder. 'Remember the first two albums with Paul Di'Anno on lead vocals. Big albums, phenomenally successful but then they replaced him with Bruce Dickinson. It didn't do them no harm. Not to mention Ozzy and Black Sabbath.'

Bernie Garvey paced the room. 'All right. I don't need a lesson in heavy metal history. I have been in this business a hell of a lot longer than you guys. At the end of the day, I am your manager and I do what is right for this band and getting rid of Jimmy Parish is not the right move. No matter what you think of him, the fans love him. As I said, I will talk with him. The band has no major engagements for the next few months apart from a few interviews. Let me see if I can get Jimmy into rehab and cleaned up. Then we will talk again. OK?'

Ricky Wilder walked to the door. 'Just fucking remember we had this conversation, Bernie. Just remember when it comes back to bite you on your fat little ass.' Ricky left the room leaving the door wide open behind him.

Joey Ellis peeped in. 'Are you finished, Bernie?'

Bernie Garvey watched the disappearing figure of Wilder and then looked at Joey. 'For now. Yes.'

Joey nodded. 'By the way, Eddie called from the hospital; Jimmy will be discharged in the morning. Good news, eh?'

Bernie didn't answer.

Later, as Bernie drove back to the hotel the band were staying at, he mulled over the earlier conversation. He knew the band's concerns about Jimmy were genuine and the points they raised were relevant but Jimmy Parish had become a rock god in the last few years. He had developed from a fledgling singer into a powerhouse, whose voice, when on point, could rival even the likes of Robert Plant or Ian Gillan in their prime. He couldn't risk losing him, plus they went back a long way and they were close friends.

Bernie knew, like many of the musical greats, Jimmy could be a sweetheart one minute, a diva the next, but also a nasty bastard with a mean streak in him. When he lost the plot, he could be dangerous. Bernie didn't relish the thought of ever having to confront him about his drug problems. He knew as a friend he had let Jimmy get away with far too much in the past but he had his private reasons for this and they needed to stay private.

As he pulled into the forecourt of the hotel, he had this niggling feeling at the back of his head that if things didn't change with Jimmy soon, the band would force his hand. If he were to kick Jimmy out the band, he shuddered at the consequences. As he got out of the car and handed his keys to the valet, he decided he was heading for the bar. He needed a good stiff drink before he could even begin to contemplate the thought of Jimmy Parish leaving the band.

Chapter 2

Two months later the band were due to appear on the Channel 4 talk show, *SATURDAY NIGHT CHAT WITH DYLAN RAMSEY.* Ramsey was a Welsh-born comedian/actor who had become a popular chat show host known for his down-to-earth and no-nonsense interviewing. This final show of the current series had Stormtrooper as top of the bill. Also on the show was Arsenal and England footballer, Gary Hale, and also current Hollywood darlings, husband and wife actors, Melissa French and Damien Curtis.

This was an exciting line-up for the closing show of another hugely successful series. The band was to close the show with their new single release, "You are my shot in the arm". Jimmy Parish and Ricky Wilder were going to be the two band members to be interviewed before the song. Ramsey and the team behind the show knew this was a massive line-up to bring the curtain down on this current series.

The band were in the green room watching the other guests being interviewed. They were far from relaxed as Jimmy had not yet arrived. This was their first engagement as a band since the Donington gig and already Jimmy was again causing them problems. Bernie had arranged an uneasy truce between Parish and Wilder so that they would get through the show which pulled in six million viewers regularly. It was a huge opportunity to plug the new single and hopefully rocket it to number one.

Bernie Garvey was out in the corridor trying to reassure the programme runner that Parish was on his way. The flustered young man, named Billy, who was gripping his clipboard tightly with white knuckles, told Garvey the band were on in under fifteen minutes. Garvey nodded his head and once more assured Billy that Parish would be here. The young man headed off down the corridor, looking worried as he spoke into a walkie talkie.

Garvey headed to a public phone in reception and dialled Jimmy's car phone. He dared not step a foot back in the green room without knowing where Jimmy was otherwise the rest of the band would slaughter him. Jimmy had recently come out of rehab but the band still collectively wanted shot of him. Bernie had managed to pacify them for the moment but he knew deep down he was only plugging the hole in the dam with his finger.

After a dozen rings, the phone was answered by a drunk-sounding Parish. 'Yeah.'

'Jimmy, it's Bernie, where the hell are you?'

'Bernie, my old mate, how is it going?'

'Don't "Bernie old mate" me, Jimmy. You are meant to be on air in fifteen minutes.'

'No sweat, Bernie. My car is just pulling up in front of the studio now.'

The phone line went dead. Bernie breathed a sigh of relief, put the receiver back in its cradle and headed to the front doors. He was just in time to see Jimmy Parish unceremoniously exit his Mercedes via the passenger side. He looked dishevelled, cowboy hat askew on his head and he had an unlit Marlboro Light dangling from his lips.

Bernie's blood boiled. The money and time spent at the Priory obviously had been a complete waste of time.

Parish stuck his head back in through the open window of the car. 'Park it up, Errol, and I will see you back here later.'

A large black man the size of a small island in the driver's seat nodded. 'OK, boss.'

Errol Allen was not only the chauffeur; he was also Jimmy's minder. At six feet, six inches and 120 kilos, not many people bothered him. He was also an ex-Olympic gold medallist in judo.

The Mercedes slid smoothly and silently away from the kerb. Jimmy then turned and saw Bernie stood in the doorway with a look of concern plastered over his face. Jimmy Parish walked unsteadily towards him. 'OK, Bernie, no need to get your Y-fronts in a knot, the cavalry has arrived.'

Bernie couldn't keep a lid on his anger any longer. 'You are pissed, you idiot. All that fucking money spent on rehab and you are drinking again as soon as you get out. For God's sake, have you got a bloody death wish? The band are being interviewed on TV's biggest chat show and are also going to close the show with the new single and you are drunk.'

Jimmy clapped his hand on Bernie's back. 'You worry too much, Bernie. I have had a few to relax and calm the nerves, that's all. I will be fine. Come on, lead the way, we don't want to be late, do we.'

Bernie gritted his teeth. He wasn't a violent man but at that moment he wanted to punch Jimmy straight in the mouth. He didn't have time to carry on with this conversation, he just hoped and prayed Jimmy would hold up. Bernie walked him to the make-up room.

'Get in there and see if you can get a cup of black coffee inside you. As soon as you are done, get up to the green room – it is at the end of this corridor on the left. Got it?'

Jimmy lifted a fake salute to his temple and grinned. 'Aye, aye, Captain.' He then disappeared inside.

Bernie headed for the green room. He knew the reception he would be likely to receive but he was running out of time so he would just override any shit for now. He opened the door to be greeted by the expectant faces of the band.

Bernie put up a hand. 'We have no time now for debate. Jimmy is here and is in make-up. He will be joining you in a few minutes.' Ricky went to speak but Bernie raised his hand again and then left the room.

Bernie almost bumped into the young runner. 'Mr Garvey, the band now need to move to the side stage. Five minutes before they are on.'

Bernie slapped a false smile on his features. 'Fine, Billy. They will be there. Jimmy is now here. All is good.'

He headed back once more to the green room. Bernie opened the door halfway. 'OK. Let's go, we're on.'

As the band left the room, Jimmy appeared from make-up. His hair had been expertly coiffured and his appearance looked perfect. A true rock god. He grinned at the approaching band. 'Hello, darlings. Shall we do this then?' With that he turned and walked off.

Ricky lent in close to Bernie. 'Please tell me he isn't drunk.'

Bernie smiled nervously. 'He has had a few, admittedly, but he will be fine.'

Ricky pushed past Bernie. 'He fucking better be.' Ricky made to move off but stopped and looked back at Bernie. 'Remember our little conversation after the Donington gig?'

Before Bernie could answer, Ricky walked away.

'Thank you for now, Melissa French and Damien Curtis, and all the best with the new film, *The Outlaws,* released here in October,' said Dylan Ramsey as the audience broke into rapturous applause.

Ramsey now faced the camera. 'In the last year, unless you have been living on the moon, you will have surely heard of the rock band, Stormtrooper. This British band has recently completed a hugely successful tour of the USA and headlined the Monsters of Rock festival at Donington. Their latest album, *Riding Shotgun,* is topping the UK and the US charts, as did their single, "Burning Ambition". At this moment in time, the band seem to have the Midas touch. Let's give a warm welcome to Jimmy Parish and Ricky Wilder of Stormtrooper.'

The audience once more erupted into wild applause as the two men walked onto the set with Jimmy Parish leading the way unsteadily. The other guests stood up to welcome them. Parish passed Damien Curtis, who offered his hand. Jimmy made to shake it but, at the last minute, cocked him a snook instead. The man was obviously taken aback. He then took Melissa French's hand and kissed the back of it before seductively licking it. Damien Curtis' face was now like thunder. Jimmy finished his entrance by throwing a playful punch in footballer Gary Hale's direction, shouting, 'Up the Spurs!' Ricky Wilder followed, choosing to shake the other guests' hands without incident and inwardly cursing Parish.

Dylan Ramsey shook both men's hands. As he shook Jimmy's, the inebriated star kissed him on the cheek. Once seated Ramsey opened the conversation. 'Well, quite an entrance, Jimmy. Although I suppose you are known for your flamboyance.'

'Am I? I wouldn't know,' answered Jimmy with a twinkle in his eye.

'So how was Donington? It must have been a great occasion to top the bill,' asked Ramsey.

Ricky intervened before Jimmy could answer. 'Yes, it was. A lot of our peers had headlined in the past. It certainly was a landmark occasion for us to also do it. The crowd were amazing.'

'You have also just conquered the States as well?'

Before Ricky could answer this time, Jimmy cut in. 'Well, it was about time these Yanks found out what real rock music was instead of all that REO Speedwagon, Journey and Toto bollocks.'

The dig at the Americans didn't go down well with Damien and Melissa. Dylan moved the conversation on, realising Jimmy was going to prove a handful even for his considerable chat show experience. 'Did you hurt yourself diving into the crowd at the end of the Donington set, Jimmy?'

'Never felt a thing, sweety.'

Damien Curtis cut in. 'Looks to me like the guy has suffered brain damage.'

There was a ripple of embarrassed laughter in the audience.

'I heard you ended up in hospital,' pressed Ramsey.

Parish ignored the question and picked up a glass of water from the table in front of him and took a sip.

He pulled a face. 'You cheapskate, Ramsey. I thought it might have been gin in here.'

The audience laughed once again uncomfortably as they realised Parish was well and truly pissed.

Damien Curtis saw his chance for revenge as Parish finished his remark. 'Maybe, Jimmy, Dylan saves the liquor for the important guests.'

Parish laughed. 'Indeed, you could be right. Sorry, what was your name again?'

The actor's face was like thunder. 'My name is Damien Curtis, buddy, and don't forget it.'

Ramsey loved a bit of tension on the show to ramp up the viewing figures but he also knew where to draw the line before things turned nasty. He tried to steer the conversation back to music. 'So, Jimmy, tell us about the latest album.'

Jimmy looked agitated. 'Excuse me one second, Dylan.' With that, Jimmy got up and moved surprisingly quickly for an intoxicated person and threw the glass of water in Curtis' face. 'You sanctimonious prick. If your acting was any more wooden you would grow roots,' he snarled.

After the initial shock, Curtis jumped up. He was a well-built guy and outweighed Jimmy by at least 15 kilos. The actor shoved Jimmy in the chest who went tumbling ungainly backwards onto the carpet.

Ricky got to his feet to help pick up Jimmy. The whole thing had turned into a nightmare. In the wings, Bernie Garvey held his head in his hands.

In the green room, the rest of the band couldn't believe what was unfolding on the television monitor. This was something different, even for Parish.

Dylan Ramsey was all smiles and trying to be the peacemaker, knowing inside he had just struck TV gold.

This incident would be played over and over again on every "television's worst moments" compilations for years to come. 'Gentlemen, come on now. There is no need for this,' he pleaded.

As Wilder pulled Parish up to his feet, the enraged lead singer shrugged off his grip. 'Get your fucking hands off me.' Jimmy Parish looked around, wild-eyed. It was obvious to all present it was more than the booze making him so erratic.

'Sit back down, Jimmy, please. Take a moment to compose yourself,' offered Ramsey.

'Fuck you, Dylan, and your show too. I don't need this,' snarled Parish. Jimmy ripped off his mic and with that, he walked off the set.

Ramsey, trying to be the consummate professional after the incident, moved on as best he could. 'Well, everybody, it looks like we have lost Jimmy, which is a pity as the band were about to close the show with their latest single. I am not quite sure what happens now.' He looked towards the footballer and jokingly asked, 'Can you sing, Gary?'

The footballer laughed uncomfortably. 'Only in the communal bath, Dylan.'

Ricky Wilder saw his opportunity and spoke up. 'No worries, Dylan. We will do the song. I can only apologise for Jimmy's crazy outburst. He seems to be a bit under the weather. Stormtrooper can carry on without him, no problem.'

Ramsey, somewhat relieved, nodded. 'Don't go away, viewers, we will be back after this short break.'

In the break, Ricky apologised to the other guests for Jimmy's behaviour and Damien Curtis popped off stage for a change of shirt. He seemed to be calm but who knew what was going through his mind.

Soon they were back on air. Dylan Ramsey, all smiles, looked into the camera. 'OK, ladies and gentlemen, after a rather abrupt end to the interview, here are Stormtrooper, minus one, with their new single, "YOU ARE MY SHOT IN THE ARM."

The rest of the guys joined Ricky over on the show's stage. Although they were all shellshocked by what had just transpired, they put on their professional faces.

The audience went wild as the band launched into the song with Ricky Wilder on the lead vocals. His voice was rich and gravelly. Different to Jimmy's. He was in total control of the show, metaphorically making love to the camera. He knew this was his moment to show the fans that he could be the frontman of the band and he was going to grab it with both hands.

If Jimmy Parish had still been in the building, he would have found cause for concern, but he wasn't. After coming off stage earlier, he had brushed passed Bernie with a mumbled "fuck off" and called to the doorman in the foyer to get his chauffeur ,Errol, and the car. 'Tell him I said to get the car around to the front, sharpish. I am out of here. I don't want to be around this shit any longer than necessary.'

He disappeared into the nearest bathroom where, in one of the toilet cubicles, he sniffed a line of cocaine off the top of the cistern. With that, he wandered back out and out of the studio. He lit up a cigarette just as the Mercedes pulled up out front.

Errol squeezed his bulk out of the driver's seat and opened the backdoor for Jimmy. 'How did it go, boss?' the big man asked.

Jimmy spilled into the backseat and then answered, 'Fucking wonderful, Errol. Fucking wonderful.' He then opened the minibar and poured himself a Jack Daniels as the car pulled away into the night.

The band finished up with Wilder blasting the vocal completely out of the water. The catchy chorus and guitar riff made this latest single surely another chart-topper. The audience and the guests applauded and cheered; all the previous commotion now seemingly forgotten. Even Damien Curtis was smiling and clapping. Ricky milked the moment. In his mind, he had just proved to the nation that he could front the band and Jimmy Parish was yesterday's news.

Backstage, Ricky found Bernie in the corridor. The pallor of the man's face was deathly white. Before Bernie could react, Ricky had grabbed him by the arm and guided him into the nearby bathroom.

Once inside, he let the man go and faced him. 'I fucking warned you, Bernie. Jimmy has been a car crash waiting to happen and now it has. You wouldn't fucking listen and now this pantomime has occurred in front of millions.

Bernie raised his hands. 'All right, Ricky. All right, for God's sake. I know. I wouldn't have believed it if I hadn't seen it with my own eyes.'

'So, Bernie, does he go?'

'Give me a moment to think. I have to—'

Ricky cut him down. 'Time for thinking is over. It is a time for doing. I saved tonight by getting out there and singing the new single and, if I say so myself, I think I fucking nailed it.'

Bernie nodded. 'It was exceptionally good, Ricky. It really was, but—'

Once again, Ricky cut in. 'No more fucking "buts". Jimmy insulted one of the biggest film actors on the planet and threw a glass of water in the man's face, for Christ's sake. I am surprised he isn't already on to his lawyers in Beverley Hills to sue the fuck out of the band. He made a complete fool out of himself, which, personally, I don't give two fucks about but it is reflecting on the rest of the band. I can't understand why you keep defending him. I have had enough. He did six weeks in the fucking Priory and manages to come out worse than when he went in. He is a lost cause. Either he goes or I do and probably the rest of the band too. You will be left with Jimmy on his own as a solo artist. See how long that will last. It is him or the band, Bernie. Fucking decision time. Can you imagine tomorrow's newspaper headlines? He will be crucified and you are going to be the joke manager that sticks by him. Get him into rehab again if you think it will do any good for his own health but where the band is concerned, he is gone.'

Bernie walked over to a row of sinks and stopped at one and turned on the cold-water tap. He leant forward and splashed water on his face and then sucked in a couple of mouthfuls. He dried his face on a paper towel and sighed deeply before facing Ricky. 'OK. He goes. I will go around his place tomorrow and tell him, but I will have to tread carefully.'

Ricky now breathed a sigh of relief. 'At long last you are seeing some sense. You won't regret this, Bernie. In a few months' time the fans won't even remember Jimmy Parish. I promise.'

Bernie managed a weak grin. 'I hope so. I really do.' The man looked defeated and tired.

'Do you fancy some back-up tomorrow when you visit him?' asked Ricky.

Bernie nodded. 'Yes please. I don't expect him to take the news lying down or to go quietly. In fact, I don't know what to expect.'

Ricky realised what Bernie had said was true. Although he knew it was the right thing to do for the band's future, he was also concerned about what Jimmy might dredge up from the past. Jimmy and Ricky had been close friends since they were young men but in recent times their relationship had gone sour. There was a lot of animosity between them now. They also held secrets about each other that were better off buried, but when anger or jealousy reared their ugly heads then things could get dangerous.

Ricky wrapped an arm around Bernie's shoulders. 'Come on, let's meet up with the rest of the lads in the studio bar and I will buy you a Baileys.'

Bernie afforded himself a small grin. 'The drinks are complimentary in the bar.'

Ricky laughed. 'Even better then. I will stand you two.'

Chapter 3

At 11.30am, Sunday morning, Bernie Garvey pulled his Range Rover into the forecourt of Jimmy Parish's country retreat, Bracknell Hall, in Berkshire. Jimmy, when he wasn't raising hell in the rock world, fancied himself as a bit of a country gent.

The people in the nearby village of Avonlea loved the fact that there was a celebrity up at the "big house". Jimmy was the talk of the village when he drove his silver ghost Rolls Royce or the smoke grey Mercedes the five-minute journey down there to buy *The Sun* newspaper and a packet of Marlboro Lights.

Bracknell Hall was an impressive Georgian nine-bedroom house, complete with swimming pool, jacuzzi, indoor cinema and games room. It was built in 1740 in the reign of George II and had been owned by the Kirby family until 1975 when the final Kirby, a John Edward, passed on with no children to inherit the property. The building had been sold to a group of property developers who were going to convert it into a health retreat but funding for the project fell through. The house lay empty until Jimmy's personal assistant, following his brief to look for a country pile, found it.

When Jimmy visited, he loved the place, and bought it straight away. He moved into it two years ago with his wife, Mary Gilmour. They had been living previously in a penthouse flat in North London but Jimmy had tired of the constant attention of the paparazzi and fans camping daily on his doorstep, so he had literally escaped to the country.

His wife, Mary, was a famous artist who had a number of galleries across the UK. She was a vivacious and clever blonde. Cambridge educated. They complemented each other, both being creative people in their chosen fields. A self portrait of Jimmy, painted by Mary, hung in the dining room over the fireplace at the hall. It was always a constant source of piss-taking when the band visited. But that was in the good old days when Stormtrooper were united. Days before Jimmy's drug-taking and boozing got out of hand.

Bernie always blamed the drug usage on Mary, who insisted that she needed to take LSD for her creative juices to flow so that she could paint freely and express herself. She had encouraged Jimmy to do likewise to help his song-writing. She often told him, if it was good enough for John Lennon it was good enough for him.

Jimmy was absolutely dedicated to Mary and wouldn't have a word said against her. He doted on her. Mary knew being a rockstar's wife was not going to be easy. She knew when Jimmy was on tour, he was going to be getting into any little groupie's panties that threw herself at him but she could live with this as long as he came home to her and he always did.

After a disastrous and volatile short-lived marriage to cocktail waitress, Trudy Henderson, when Jimmy was 20 years of age, which ended after 12 weeks, his relationship now was completely different. He was head over heels in love with Mary and she with him. All was happy on the home front. There was even talk of trying for a family.

Bernie turned the engine off and both him and Ricky sat and surveyed the house. All was quiet except for the chirping of birds in the trees that surrounded the gardens. It had taken him roughly 90 minutes to travel across from London. Traffic had been light as it was Sunday. Thrown on the back seat of the vehicle were half a dozen Sunday newspapers. All the front pages were about Jimmy's outburst and appalling behaviour on the Dylan Ramsey show. The negative press had only cemented the case for the sacking of Parish.

'How are you going to play this, Bernie?' asked Ricky.

Bernie looked nervous. 'Well, when he sees us both on the doorstep, he has got to know we aren't here to congratulate him on a successful TV appearance. I suggest I just get to the point and have done. Whatever I say, he isn't going to like it.'

Ricky grinned ruefully. 'On that I do agree with you, Bernie. Come on, let's get this over and done with.'

Bernie regarded Ricky with a look of deep concern etched on his tired features. 'I really can't believe we are doing this, Ricky.'

Ricky looked at Bernie. He suddenly looked like a vulnerable old man. 'Come on, Bernie. This isn't the time to lose your bottle. Let's go.'

Both men got out of the Range Rover and began to walk towards the house. Their footsteps sounded loud as they crunched on the gravel of the forecourt. They walked up the three steps to the front door and Ricky rang the bell. The door chime was the tune, "Tough Love" from the band's debut album, *Stormtrooper.*

Somewhere within the walls of the house, they heard movement and voices. After what seemed an eternity, the door opened and there stood a sleepy and tousle-haired Mary dressed in a baggy nightshirt. Even in this befuddled state, there was no getting away from the fact she was a beautiful-looking woman.

'Yes?' she said, with no apparent recognition of the two men on her doorstep.

'Morning, Mary,' said Bernie. 'It's me, Bernie Garvey, and Ricky Wilder. Can we have a chat with Jimmy?'

For a moment, Mary's features stayed blank and then recognition dawned. 'Oh, shit, sorry, Bernie, for acting such a dumb bitch. Had a bit of a late night here. Come on in. I will let him know you are here; he is just in the shower.' She then glanced at Ricky. 'I suppose you better come in as well.'

She turned and walked away; the two men followed, shutting the door behind them. Mary headed towards the elegant oak staircase and pointed to her left. 'Go on into the lounge. I will go get him and then rustle up some coffee.'

Both men stood inside the expansive room. A huge marble fireplace was the showcase of the lounge, with the picture windows looking out onto the drive coming a close second. Elaborate cornicing decorated the ceilings and an intricate picture rail surrounded the middle of the walls. Although the room had kept its Georgian architecture, Jimmy and Mary had added a flourish of contemporary furnishings and a large bulky television sat in the corner, complete with the latest state-of-the-art VCR recorder. In the other corner was a monstrous hi-fi stack with a million buttons and knobs on it. It resembled something you might find on a spaceship. A few of Mary's paintings adored the walls, along with a classic print of Robert Plant, the iconic lead singer of the legendary Led Zeppelin. Jimmy's idol.

Bernie regarded Ricky. 'When he comes in, I will do the talking. You're like a red rag to a bull where Jimmy's concerned. If I am to make him see sense, I am in charge. OK?'

Ricky nodded. 'I am happy with that as long as you don't lose your nerve and fall for his flannel.'

Bernie held up a hand. 'Trust me I am not going to lose my nerve. I haven't mentioned it to you yet but last night, Stardust, our American record label, rang me and told me in no uncertain terms to terminate Jimmy's contract. They saw a tape of the Ramsey debacle and said Jimmy was an embarrassment to the label and generally insulting to the American fans. Furthermore, if I didn't sort it then they would pull out of our record deal across the pond. That could be potentially devastating and we would lose millions.'

'Fucking hell, Bernie. That is not what we have all worked for. We are on the brink of something colossal and we cannot fuck it up.'

'I agree, Ricky. I admit I have been soft on Jimmy in the past but, believe me, I have my reasons, but this time I can't afford to be. We lose the American deal and we are dead in the water. Trust me, I have to follow this through.'

'Follow what through, Bernie?' Jimmy Parish had entered the room unnoticed.

Bernie Garvey and Ricky Wilder both turned around to see a dishevelled-looking Jimmy stood in the doorway. He wore a garish leopard print dressing gown and a pair of fluffy pink slippers. His hair was wet and tied back in a ponytail. He had a crystal glass tumbler in his hand containing a good measure of what looked like whisky and an unlit Marlboro Light dangled from his lips.

'Morning, Jimmy,' said Bernie.

Jimmy walked into the room. 'So, what do I owe the pleasure of this visit, may I ask?'

Bernie glanced at Ricky and then quickly said, 'Your car crash appearance on television last night. You made a complete and utter prick out of yourself.'

Jimmy took a sip of his drink. 'Really? I thought I gave everybody some great TV.'

'Well, our record label in the States didn't think so. Apart from coming over as an arrogant sod, you insulted the two American guests to boot.'

'Banter, Bernie. Just a bit of banter and rock 'n' roll glitz. No real harm done.'

Ricky Wilder walked forward. 'No real harm done? Stardust are threatening to pull the plug on our record deal, you pratt.'

Jimmy paused, mid-sip of his whisky. 'Is this right, Bernie?'

'Yes, it is. That is the icing on the cake, along with all your other fuck-ups.'

Jimmy's eyes narrowed. 'What do you mean "the icing on the cake"?'

Bernie took a deep breath. 'If your contract isn't terminated with the band forthwith, they pull the record deal and the next tour.'

Jimmy smiled nervously. 'So, what did you tell them, Bernie?'

Bernie walked over to one of the large windows and looked out on the grounds. He noticed that it was beginning to rain. Jimmy walked towards him, giving

Ricky a death stare as he passed him. 'I asked, Bernie, what you said to them?'

The question hung heavy in the air. Bernie finally turned around. 'I told them that your contract would be terminated and you would leave the band.'

'Are you fucking crazy, Bernie? There is no Stormtrooper without Jimmy Parish. I am the beating heart of the band. Fans love me, for Christ's sake.' He glanced at Ricky. 'None of the band are choirboys. You all have had your share of gear over the years, you hypocritical prick. Who are you to judge me?' He now looked back to Bernie. 'You go back and tell those asshole record boys that if I go, the band is effectively finished anyway.'

Bernie cut in. 'Maybe a year ago I would have agreed with you, Jimmy. But not now your drug habit has made you unpredictable. You are forgetting your lyrics and timing and your song-writing ability is going down the pan with your health. You are no longer in the long-term future of the band.'

Jimmy took another gulp of his drink. 'All right, so answer me this. Who is going to front the band? Have you got a big name lined up? Well? Who is it? Dickinson, Halford, Gillan?'

'Ricky will be taking on the lead vocals; we have another guitarist ready to come in.'

Jimmy laughed out loud. 'Ricky! Fucking Ricky! What is this, some sort of wind up?'

Bernie's face was grim. 'No wind up. It's happening.'

Jimmy swallowed the rest of his drink and then hurled the glass across the room to smash against the wall. 'You fucking Judas!' he screamed. He turned to Ricky. 'And as for you, you smug prick. You got some bollocks. You have some fucking big shoes to fill, my son.'

Ricky smiled. 'Yeah, and an even fucking bigger head. You are yesterday's news, Jimmy. You're all washed up.'

'Oh yeah? We will see about that.' Jimmy came forward and swung a punch in Ricky's direction.

Ricky easily sidestepped him and dropped his own punch into Jimmy's stomach. The man dropped to his knees, coughing and wheezing for breath. Ricky looked down at the fallen man who used to be his friend. What had happened to him?

Ricky had met Jimmy at Goldsmiths University in Lewisham, London, where they were both students and had instantly become friends. The had both been born and grew up in the area. At one stage, they both fancied themselves as the next Andy Warhol, but the truth was neither of them had the talent or inclination.

They hit it off immediately because of their love for music. Particularly rock. And also their passion for smoking weed. They formed a band with a couple of others and played at uni functions, before branching out to local pubs and clubs. Back then, they went under the name of Chameleon as they mainly performed covers.

Gradually, as their popularity grew, Wilder and Parish began writing their own songs. Parish usually with the lyrics and Wilder, adding the music. Both dropped out of uni to actively pursue a career in the music world.

Back then, they were like brothers. They shared everything even down to girlfriends, which got them into trouble on more than one occasion. But they were tight and watched each other's backs. Even back then, when the band puffed a little weed and enjoyed some liquor, Jimmy was already beginning to experiment with harder stuff.

As the band grew, they changed their name and personnel. They became TNT, playing mostly now their own brand of heavy rock. Finally, they were spotted by Bernie Garvey who managed some big bands in the late sixties and early seventies and was a respected "face" in the industry. He signed them up in 1977 and got them their first record deal.

On Bernie's recommendation, they changed their name to Stormtrooper in homage to the massively successful film of that year, *Star Wars*. He told them people would connect with the name. He was right the band became an overnight sensation. Their debut album that year the self-titled *Stormtrooper* went to number two in the British chart and the main single from the album, "Tough Love", hit the number one spot for four weeks. They supported the big bands of the time Thin Lizzy, Rainbow, Purple, and such like. Their reputation grew.

The rest, you could say, is history. But in the last year, things had taken a turn for the worst, now resulting in this moment.

'You have brought this on yourself, Jimmy. You were warned enough times.'

Jimmy clambered up to one knee. 'Fuck off out of my house now. If you think I am going to take this lying down, you have another thing coming. I will get my solicitors on to this.'

Bernie stepped closer. 'I am sorry that it has come to this, Jimmy. But I have to think of the big picture and the band's future.'

Jimmy grimaced. 'Thinking of lining your fucking pockets as well.'

Bernie nodded to Ricky. It was time to leave. Both men walked to the door.

Bernie looked back as Jimmy flopped down onto the sofa. 'You will get what you are owed and you will still get royalties for your songs. Legally, you haven't got a leg to stand on after your performances and drug dependency. If you had read the small print of your contract, you will have seen you have broken a number of the clauses in it.'

Jimmy looked up. He looked a beaten man but then a smile played on his lips. 'Are you both really sure you want to do this? I won't go quietly and I know shit about you both. I could go to the newspapers and sell my story.'

Bernie and Ricky exchanged nervous glances. Ricky then spoke. 'All water under the bridge, buddy. Hearsay and lies. It's the past. The band's lawyers will destroy you. You could risk losing everything, including this place. Is it really worth it?'

Jimmy seemed to mull this over. He then exploded with anger once more. 'Fuck off and stick your contract up your ass, Bernie. You would probably enjoy that, I suspect.' He regarded Ricky with disdain. 'You, brother, I am disappointed in. I thought we looked after each other's backs, no matter what. We had a pact.'

Ricky replied, 'Once, Jimmy. But now you are too much of a risk to all the band has built. I can't risk losing it all for you. You have gone too far. I wish you no harm personally; this is purely business.'

'If I am going down, it won't be quietly, I promise I will take you with me. No Jimmy Parish, no Stormtrooper. You can bet your life on that.'

Both men had heard enough. They could do no more. They hoped Jimmy would calm down and think things over in a day or two. They turned and walked out of the room just as Mary appeared with a tray of cups in her hands. She looked surprised.

'Going so soon? I just made some coffee.'

Bernie smiled weakly. 'Sorry, love, we are in a hurry.'

She looked towards Jimmy for an explanation. He sat on the edge of the sofa with his head in his hands.

Outside the front door, Bernie breathed a sigh of relief. 'Jesus Christ, that was tough going.'

Ricky clapped him on the back. 'You played a blinder, Bernie. Now let's get on with making Stormtrooper world-beaters.

'Do you not feel any remorse?' asked Bernie.

'I am truly sorry it had to come to this. I hope to God Jimmy sorts himself out but he is not the man I used to know anymore. The band's future and our own personal futures take precedence over sentimentality.'

As they walked towards the Range Rover, the front door of the house opened and Jimmy ran out. He was now wearing his black tombstone cowboy hat. Both men glanced back as they walked and immediately saw the gun in his hand. Jimmy was an avid collector of firearms and fascinated by the Wild West. At the moment, he was wielding a vintage Colt .45.

'You won't last a fucking minute without me, you pair of backstabbing bastards. I have dirt on all of you and I will go to the media and tell them. I promise you. You are nothing without me. Bernie, I know about you. I could ruin you and your family.'

The older man's face blanched. He knew this would happen; that's why he had been so reluctant to sack Jimmy.

Jimmy continued, 'And you, Ricky my son, I can destroy you. Remember Dublin '79? Sure you do. How could you forget?'

Ricky stopped in his tracks. A shudder ran down his spine as he looked back at Jimmy. He hadn't heard that mentioned in a long time. In fact, Jimmy and he made a pact never to mention it again, way back. 'If you reveal it, we both will suffer. What is the point?'

Jimmy grinned crazily. 'Because I fucking can. Because I can, Ricky.'

Ricky went to say something but then Bernie Garvey and he saw Jimmy drunkenly trying to level the gun in their direction.

Ricky shouted, 'Time to run, Bernie!'

As both men broke into an enforced sprint, the gun went off, taking the head off a stone statue of a Bacchus, the Greco-Roman god of wine, stood by an ornamental fountain. Luckily, it was nowhere near them. Jimmy, still nursing the mother of all hangovers wasn't going to hit anything of note that day.

As they dived into the Range Rover and Bernie started it up, another bullet with more luck than judgement put out the right-side headlight.

'That crazy bastard is certifiable. Quick, put your boot down,' shouted Ricky.

As they pulled away in a shower of gravel, Bernie glanced in the rear-view mirror and saw Mary appear and wrestle the gun from Jimmy's hands.

Only in the world of rock 'n' roll, thought Bernie as they sped out of the gateway to safety.

Chapter 4

Sometime later

As promised, after the initial surprise in some quarters, outrage in others, Stormtrooper went from strength to strength. The 21-year-old Marshall Meyers from Texas came on board. His blonde hair and baby-faced looks were an instant hit with the ladies. Also, his guitar-playing made him sound like a burgeoning Eddie Van Halen. Ricky took to lead vocals like a duck to water.

Their first album post Jimmy Parish, *From the Ashes,* steamed its way once more to the top of the charts in Great Britain and across the Atlantic. The first single from the album, called "Empty Promises", also went to number one on both sides of the pond. The spectre of Jimmy Parish was gradually fading away and the "mark 2" line-up of the band were even bigger than the original.

As for Jimmy, he lost a bitter court battle over his sacking and contractual rights. It only fuelled his hatred for the band, and particularly Ricky Wilder, but his threats of exposing the band had yet to materialise. The band's legal team were ready and poised if they did.

He started his own band, Jimmy Parish's Inferno. After moderate success with his debut album, the next one flopped. Mainly this was because the album was well overdue for release but also Jimmy's voice was fading fast. Also, his drug habit had got worst. The band split acrimoniously as Jimmy just wasn't writing any material.

He was given a break when iconic UK heavy metal band, Iron Fist, asked him to stand in for their lead vocalist, Brett Rodgers, who had come down with a bout of hepatitis and couldn't complete their European tour. Jimmy did the first two dates in Munich and Cologne and then went missing in action somewhere in the Bierkellers and red-light district of Berlin for two weeks. He was sacked and luckily Rob Halford of Judas Priest stepped in to save the day.

Jimmy Parish was now a pariah. Everybody steered well clear of him. There was no work forthcoming. He became a virtual recluse at Bracknell Hall, with him and Mary both slipping further into a self-fuelled drug-addled existence. Occasionally he was seen in the media coming out of a nightclub, worse for wear, and brawling with a photographer or tabloid journalist. Even this now was becoming a bit old hat.

As this was happening, Stormtrooper had completed another successful stateside tour, climaxing with two sell-out shows at Madison Square Gardens, New York. This was followed by a tour of the Far East and they released a live double album entitled *Storm over Tokyo*. The public and music press loved it.

The band could do no wrong and even die-hard fans of the band from day one were not talking about Jimmy as much as they used to as Ricky Wilder had risen to become one of the best frontmen in the world, being mentioned in the same breath as his contemporaries such as Bruce Dickinson and Steven Tyler.

Jimmy's drug habit got to the point where he had to be rushed into hospital before the New Year of '87. He nearly died but was saved by the brilliant medical team. After leaving hospital, he went into rehab for three months. He came out clean and healthier.

The music press, realising that the year previously, the legendary frontman of Thin Lizzy, Phil Lynott, had suddenly died from a drug-related illness without any fanfare, they panicked, thinking they were about to lose another rock god, albeit a flawed one.

When Jimmy had fully recovered, a publishing house offered him a lucrative deal to write a "warts and all" book about his career and his time in the band. It was the lifeline that Jimmy desperately needed as he was near to bankruptcy after the court case and also stupid business deals that had fell through. He was also in danger of losing his precious Bracknell Hall.

So Jimmy promised the publishers he would reveal all and leave no stone unturned. He was prepared to dish the dirt on all involved with the band. When Stormtrooper's management team, Bernie Garvey and the band heard the news, they were far from impressed. With what had transpired between them and Parish over the last few years they knew he would try to hang them out to dry as some sort of warped revenge and wouldn't worry if the stories were made up or true. Whatever he was planning on publishing or saying could potentially ruin the band's reputation.

At first, they tried to strike a deal with the publishers, with no success, and then secondly tried to get the book banned. They claimed whatever was being proposed to be written would be prejudiced against them as the split between them and Jimmy had been so bitter.

This avenue was also unsuccessful as a court ruling told them they could not ban something that was yet to be written. To try and legally block the book, it would first have to be published. This was not what Stormtrooper wanted to hear.

When Jimmy got the publishing deal through, he started putting some rough notes together in a journal. With Mary and himself both being sober, it helped him focus and an outline of the book began to appear. The plan was for a ghost writer to eventually be hired to come in and record conversations and write the final draft.

A week later was his 26th birthday and he decided to hold a party aboard his 40-foot luxury yacht, *Sea Wolf*. Mary went down with the flu so couldn't attend. She was worried Jimmy might succumb to temptation so she warned him to be careful but she was also wary that she didn't want to spoil his mood as he seemed at his happiest for a long time.

His yacht was moored in Brighton on the south coast of Sussex. Jimmy who could sail the yacht himself took it out 20 miles from shore into the English Channel and anchored it there. He invited 20 or so close friends who had stayed by him in his rough times and had helped him out in his professional and private life. He also brought on board catering staff and a Michelin-starred chef. As his friends tucked into good food and wine, Jimmy stuck to mineral water, resisting temptation.

He lasted an hour before he sank his first Jack Daniels on the rocks in the company of TV comedian, Johnnie Jessup. An old mate and hard drinker. Four more bourbons and a line of coke had Jimmy in full party mode. His sobriety was now forgotten as his bloodstream took on the cocktail of alcohol and cocaine. Why not, he thought, he had earnt it. Come tomorrow, he would get back on the wagon and Mary would be none the wiser.

He was excited about the publishing contract. He had waited for his revenge and now it was coming. This book, with its explosive revelations about each and every member of the band and the management, would burst their fucking balloon and bring them back down to earth with a bump. The bastards deserved it for kicking him into touch. This would be the nail in the coffin for Stormtrooper. OK, there might be some artistic license included in his anecdotes, but who cared. The publishers were only interested in selling copies and he assured them they would.

He had been painted as the only bad boy in the band but that was not the case. Everybody had a skeleton or two rattling around in their closet. These days, the band acted squeaky clean for the masses and had become all self-righteous. The sanctimonious bastards. But when the band was on tour across the world, those long, lonely nights would be filled with booze, drugs, sex and other debauchery. Stormtrooper, at their height, had made Mötley Crüe look like schoolboys. You couldn't keep any secrets at such close proximity to each other.

Jimmy hadn't always been so stoned that he hadn't listened. When it came to Ricky, they went way back. He couldn't believe he had turned on him. They had known each other from boys of 18 years of age. They had experienced a lot of shit together, good and bad. He never thought Ricky would become a Judas but his greed and ambition had got the better of him and now he had to pay. The story of Dublin 1979 would be told.

He knew the band's lawyers had been campaigning hard to stop the publishing of the book, although they weren't sure exactly what was going to be in it. The preorder interest for the book was huge, even though a word hadn't officially been written yet. There was a lot of money at stake.

The previous night, he had been surprised to receive a phone call from Ricky. They hadn't spoke for two years or more. Nobody from the band had been near him, even when he had been rushed to hospital that New Year's Eve. Not one of the miserable bastards had so much as visited him with a lousy bunch of grapes.

He was persuaded to answer the phone call by Mary against his better judgement. The call, as he had suspected, hadn't been amiable. Ricky wanted to know what Jimmy was going to print about him. What secrets was he going to spill. Jimmy refused to tell him anything. He just dangled the carrot of possibilities in front of Wilder. He had him rattled, for sure, and that was exactly what he had planned. As Ricky's pleas became threats, Jimmy had hung up on him.

The party on the boat went on to the small hours of the morning until everybody finally crashed. The caterers and chef went back to land by speedboat hired for them. Jimmy was left on his own. The last man standing. He had just had a conversation with somebody who he had seen around the party but couldn't remember their name. Both of them had been pretty wasted.

Jimmy decided to take one final drink up onto the deck. He unsteadily made his way up there. He walked to the edge of the boat and looked out across the water. The stars in the clear night sky sparkled like a million diamonds. The full moon illuminated the sea in a silvery glow. He raised a glass to the heavens. 'Thank you, God, for being in my corner for once. I think my life is finally back on the up. I will finish this drink and then get my head down. Tomorrow I am back on the wagon.'

Suddenly the lights went out on deck. *WTF,* Jimmy thought as he looked around. The moon had slipped behind a cloud momentarily and he could see very little. Jimmy then heard a noise behind him. He turned around, stumbling slightly. 'who's there? Is that you, Benny?'

Benny Elliot was Jimmy's personal assistant. He had been responsible for finding Bracknell Hall for him and had been a loyal friend for years. When he had a few drinks in him, he could be a bit of a practical joker though.

'Switch those bloody lights back on, you clown, and stop fucking about,' said Jimmy. Jimmy walked towards the bow of the boat treading carefully over disregarded plastic bottles and glasses left by the party revellers. 'Come on, the joke's over. Light up the deck. I am off to bed and can't see fuck all.'

As Jimmy reached the bow, he grabbed the edge of the boat to steady himself as a swell of the sea rocked it around. He looked over the side of the yacht and was puzzled to see a small motorised dingy tied up. It wasn't the *Sea Wolf's* life raft. What the hell was that doing there? He didn't recognise it. As Jimmy regarded the lone dingy through blurry eyes, he was hit a heavy blow to the back of his skull, which resulted in him going over the side, into the water.

The next morning, when everybody finally rose from their sleep on the yacht, Jimmy was nowhere to be seen.

The yacht had somehow lifted anchor and drifted miles away from its original mooring. After disposing of any incriminating drug evidence into the sea, one of the guests radioed in for help and eventually the harbour master brought the police out to *Sea Wolf*. There was no sign of Jimmy anywhere on the yacht. Had he fallen over the side in a drunken stupor?

The twenty guests were all interviewed but all of them reported the same thing – that they had all crashed out and, up until then, Jimmy was still partying.

A young man named Jeremy Fuller was supposedly the last man to see Jimmy Parish, at around 2am. He told the police that Jimmy was still wide awake and drinking at that time in the galley. Jeremy told them as he decided to crash out Jimmy was heading for the deck. Possibly somebody else could have been awake somewhere else on the boat but he couldn't swear to it.

The yacht was thoroughly searched but nothing untoward was discovered. The boat's life raft was still intact so nobody had left on it. The surrounding waters were combed for a body but nothing was ever found. It was a large expanse of sea and as the boat had drifted, it was a nigh on impossible job.

The harbour master told the police that if Jimmy had drowned, the corpse would eventually come to the surface due to methane and other gases in the body, which would bloat and inflate it. The body never did resurface.

After weeks of investigation, it was finally put down to a tragic accident. An open verdict was left on the case.

Mary Gilmour was devastated when she found out the news. Since Jimmy had been rushed to hospital after overdosing, they had both cleaned up their act and their lives had been better for it. Jimmy had even started writing a few new songs and talked about forming a new band. She hadn't imagined for one minute Jimmy would relapse to this extent. Mary had been concerned when Jimmy had suggested the party but she had put her trust in him. Look where that had got her. Guests had revealed to her that Jimmy had been drinking and taking cocaine. Worst of all was the fact she had been waiting on his return to give him the good news that he was to become a father as she was carrying his unborn child. She hadn't told him the news until she was sure all was OK from her ten-week hospital appointment and then she had gone down with the flu. Now her whole world overnight had shattered. Jimmy Parish. The lovable rogue, fallen rock god and hellraiser, was dead.

A ceremony was held on the deck of the *Sea Wolf* at the exact spot it had been anchored on the night of his death. A simple service was delivered and flowers were thrown into the sea. It was all very low key for such a big personality.

Mary gave birth on September 20th, 1989, to a healthy six-pound, 4-ounce baby girl, who she named Eve. But, suffering from post-natal depression and missing Jimmy terribly, she went back to drugs. Social services became involved and eventually had to take the baby away to foster care. At this stage Mary was incapable of doing anything about it. Mary went into the rehab to try and recover so that she could have Eve back.

When she came out, clean and sober, she expected to have her child returned to her but that wasn't how it worked. She had to stay clean for six months or more and then the legal system would review her case. Sadly, two months later, at the age of 26, she died from a massive overdose of LSD after she had a relapse. She was found three days after her death by the gardener at Bracknell Hall who had looked through the dining room window after failing to get anybody to answer the front door after several tries. Mary Gilmour was slumped facedown at the dining table. It was a tragic ending chapter to both Jimmy and Mary's young lives. Both victims of excess and addiction.

Baby Eve never got a chance to know her birth mother or father and was permanently put into the foster care programme.

The band heard about Jimmy's death whilst they were touring Australia. They had been saddened by the news but not overly shocked simply because it had been Jimmy and he had slowly but surely been heading towards self-destruction. Also, they inwardly breathed a sigh of relief as the proposed book was now history. Bernie organised a wreath in the shape of a massive guitar to be sent to the ceremony from the band.

They had returned back to England sometime later when they then learnt of Mary's death. Bernie, once again, as a sign of respect, sent another wreath to her funeral but none of the band attended. They now wanted to distance themselves from these tragic events and move on.

Stormtrooper carried on their huge success, seeing the 80s out with another number one album of their greatest hits entitled *Storming Tracks*. This was to be their last top 10 success. The early 90s brought to our shores the grunge music movement, which started in Seattle, Washington. The likes of Nirvana, Alice in Chains and Pearl Jam stormed the airwaves and the charts.

Heavy metal began to become yesterday's news to the younger generation and its popularity began to wane. Although Stormtrooper had a loyal fan base, they found it difficult to recapture the magic of those golden years in the 80s. They plodded on with more album releases but now they were struggling to break the top 20 of the single and album charts.

The music scene was changing rapidly. Vinyl had been replaced, firstly by cassette tapes, which had, in turn, began to be replaced with CDs. There was also talk now of downloadable music. The days of fans pouring over an album cover and inner sleeve notes were all but gone. Independent record stores were beginning to shut down all over the place as vinyl was becoming a thing of the past.

Ricky Wilder was finding it difficult to come by writing inspiration. Things had gone stale. Some of the band members talked about pursuing solo projects or having time out. On the back of these discussions, Stormtrooper decided, on the 19th of June, 2000 to break up after a hell of a ride that saw them enter into the ROCK 'N' ROLL HALL OF FAME. They would go down in music history as one of the most successful UK rock bands ever.

In subsequent years, when the band members were interviewed, the subject of Jimmy Parish always came up and so did the conspiracy theories as to what actually happened to him. Some stories suggested he was murdered by drug dealers he owed money to. Some said it was an unfortunate accident. Others said he faked his own death to disappear from the limelight. To back up this theory, just like Elvis Presley, Jimmy had been spotted everywhere, from sunbathing on a beach in Rio de Janeiro to driving a yellow taxi cab in New York to working behind the counter in the HMV megastore on Oxford Street. The hardcore fans of the "mark 1" version of the band didn't want to believe their idol was gone. Just as fans still mourned the loss of musical geniuses like Freddie Mercury, Bolan and Morrison, for some, Jimmy Parish would be held in the same esteem.

For the rest of the band, particularly Ricky Wilder and Bernie Garvey, they just wished the subject would be closed once and for all. Whatever had happened to Jimmy on his yacht that night had been a stroke of luck for the band, as none of their own private secrets had been revealed in the intended book. When they eventually split, their reputation was intact and their place in rock history cemented forever. It had been a rollercoaster ride when rock 'n' roll ruled the airwaves and heavy metal music was king.

In the coming years, the band were offered on more than one occasion the chance to reform and play some concerts but they resisted the temptation and the big money offers. They all moved on to other projects, not all within the music industry, and gradually they moved out of the public eye. It was an end of an era. They would now live off the royalties.

Chapter 5

Present day, 2022

Ricky Wilder gazed out of the window of the plane as the rain lashed against it. The aircraft bumped up and down in the turbulence created by the current storm. He had never been a great fan of flying at the best of times but in this plane, that held only 19 passengers, things were certainly hairier, especially in this atrocious weather. Ricky looked around at the others on the plane and sensed they would all be happier when they were on the ground.

A voice from the cockpit announced they were now preparing to descend to land and they should be down in 10 minutes. Ricky breathed a sigh of relief and finished off his Jack Daniels on the rocks.

The pilot's name was Liam Foster; he was a seasoned flyer. For years he had flown documentary crews into some of the most remote places on the planet. He was known in showbusiness circles as one of the best flyers around.

The plane he was flying was a Viking DHC-6-400 Twin Otter. It was capable of carrying passengers and cargo into some of the world's most inhospitable locations. The plane was built to operate in the harshest of environments, from sub-zero Antarctica and the hottest deserts of North Africa to the mountains of the Himalayas.

He was descending into the remote Outer Hebrides, which lay 40 miles north-west of mainland Scotland, to land at a small airport on the island of Benbecula which was one of the westerly isles. There were 15 inhabited islands in the Outer Hebrides, the largest being Lewis and Harris. There were also 50 uninhabited. It was one of the uninhabited islands the passengers on this plane would eventually go to.

The plane had flew from Glasgow. It was roughly a 55-minute flight covering 177 miles. All the way from Glasgow it had endured a bumpy flight due to the storm that had followed it. This part of Great Britain had been experiencing some terrible weather in the last week, with torrential rain and high winds resulting in much flooding, structural damage, and general chaos. The latest weather forecast said there was worse to come. Storm Alec was supposedly on its way across the Atlantic towards the British Isles within the next 48 hours.

Liam had got the go-ahead to proceed with his journey from the flight tower in Glasgow, informing him he had around a two-hour window between storms to get to his destination. Unfortunately, as it often proved, it was hard to fully predict the island's weather patterns, which could be temperamental to say the least.

Now Foster could just make out the lights of the runway and began his descent. He would be glad to get the plane on terra firma and deliver his passengers safely to the island. He had been told they were famous. To Foster, they just looked like a bunch of old hippies.

Apparently, back in the 80s, they were some big deal. They were a rock band called Stormtrooper. He had to look them up on Wikipedia to find out exactly who they were. They had recently reformed and were flying into this remote location to record their first studio album since 1997.

Foster was more of a U2 and Foo Fighters fan. Eighties heavy metal was not his thing. His father, Benny, who was 78 years old, knew them though and had even dug out a couple of old vinyl 33s to show him. He went on to tell Liam that he had seen the original line-up of the band in 1982 at the legendary Rainbow Theatre in Finsbury Park, London, not long before it closed down.

As the plane landed – surprisingly smoothly under the circumstances – all the passengers let out a collective shout of "hooray".

Liam Foster's voice came over the intercom.

'Ladies and gentlemen, we have landed safely. I can confirm the rain has now stopped and the winds are dying down a little. Apologies for the rough ride and I hope you have a safe onward journey. Thank you.'

Bernie Garvey stood up from his seat. His face looked ashen. 'OK, guys, thank God we have landed. What a fucking flight. Here we all are together after 20-odd years and with the promise of making a few quid and I thought we were all going to perish in the North Sea.'

'You fucking old woman, Bernie. Take another couple of Prozac; you will be fine,' said Rory Doyle.

'Piss off, Rory. I never listen to a bass player. They have no class.' A magazine sailed pass Bernie's head.

These days, the bleached blonde hair had now gone, replaced with the silver fox look. At 72, he was a little more conservative in his appearance. He was still sprightly for his age and his mind as sharp as ever. Since the band split up, he had gone on to manage a few others but never hit the heights again that he had with Stormtrooper.

He had, in recent times, been a judge on the reality music show, *The Next Best Thing*, for a few series but, in his opinion, never found anybody remotely near the next best thing. He had only done it for the pay cheque. He had no interest in being a Simon Cowell figure.

For the last 10 years, he had been living on the island of Jersey, essentially retired and winding down with his wife, Kim, his soulmate and rock of 30 years. That had all changed though when he had received an unexpected phone call from Ricky Wilder some six months ago.

Stormtrooper were being asked to reform for a charity gig named "BRITISH METAL LEGENDS BATTLE COVID". Bands such as Iron Maiden, Thunder, Saxon, Judas Priest and Def Leppard, amongst others, were also allegedly being approached. The money raised would go to the NHS in the wake of the terrible COVID pandemic which was now finally coming under control. This was a much-anticipated gig. For the diehard fans, heavy metal had never gone away, but in the mainstream, it was nearly non-existent.

But then, in the early 2000s, a British band from Lowestoft named The Darkness rekindled interest in the genre with their catchy tongue-in-cheek rock songs. Their debut album, *Permission to Land*, and their first single, "I Believe in a Thing Called Love", were a global success. On the back of this, metal had a rebirth and many bands of the 70s and 80s started touring again to sell-out shows.

The massive fan base was still there from a generation that had adored real music and proper bands that could sing, play and not lip sync. They were the generation that bought vinyl and had an encyclopaedic knowledge of the bands they followed. A generation that would proudly dig out their tour t-shirts or cut-off denim jackets emblazoned in iconic patches of rock bands whenever they attended a gig. Now their children also wanted to see these legendary groups and, by popular demand, they got it.

The "mark 2" line up reformed and played at the gig held in the grounds of the magnificent Longleat House in Wiltshire to massive acclaim. On the back of this they embarked on a successful "greatest hits" UK and European tour. They went down a storm (excuse the pun).

Talk came around to the band reforming more permanently and releasing some new material. The break had made the band members hungry once more. So, refreshed and eager, if not a little older, they signed a record deal to make a new album. The music press and the public loved the idea and couldn't wait for some new songs from the band.

They had all received a decent amount of solo success with various projects. Ricky having the most by recently appearing in series five of the smash Netflix crime show, *Above the Law*, where he played the character Marty Isles, a corrupt nightclub owner involved in sex trafficking. He had received rave reviews for his acting.

Rory had stayed in music with his own three-piece band, Lone Wolf. Marshall also stayed in the industry, playing guitar on many records of well-known stars including Michael Jackson and Prince. Erik went back to his native Norway and had taken up writing.

At present, he had four crime novels published. He was being hailed as Norway's answer to the Swede, Stieg Larsson. There was even talk of one of the books being made into a film. Ray had moved to California and found a new career selling vintage motorbikes.

The lure of making some new music had brought them all back together on the plane to the Outer Hebrides. Bernie had come up with the perfect location to record. It was an island 25 miles west of the Isle of Benbecula, where they had landed.

The island was called Ruma. The area covered 104 km^2. It had been uninhabited supposedly since Bronze Age times until the 19th century when Victorian shipping magnate and philanthropist, George Wallace, decided to build a secret bolthole for himself and his family in the form of a 20-bedroom manor house. He proposed to build the house on top of an old Bronze Age burial ground. At first, there was some resistance from historians for building on such a potentially important site. But money talks and Wallace got his way and built his dream hideaway.

The island also housed a collection of prehistoric Callanish stones that predated the famous Stonehenge. Wallace liked to peddle to his guests the legend that the seven stones that formed a circle were seven dancers who defied the powers and were tricked by the devil to dance on the Sabbath and were punished by being turned to stone. This was a romantic tale but the stones predated Christianity by a long way.

The house was reputedly haunted because of the burial ground. This didn't faze Wallace. In fact, it intrigued him as he had a passing interest in the occult and the spirit world. But he was somewhat superstitious and built two circular turret towers at each end of the house. The origin of building circular rooms was so that the devil couldn't hide in the corners.

The house became the family residence and different generations lived there over the years but, finally, the latest family member, the playboy millionaire, Scott Wallace, decided to sell the property as he spent most of his time in the south of France.

Reclusive and eccentric former film director, Harvey Barnes, bought the house 10 years ago for 4.5 million. Barnes was born in Boston, Massachusetts, but his mother had been Scottish, originally from Inverness. He held an affinity with the area. He loved its wild and rugged scenery, plus its chequered past. Barnes also funded a project to introduce pheasant, quail and partridge to the island for hunting purposes. He had an impressive gun collection at the house, including a pair of mint condition Purdy 12-gauge shotguns reportedly costing around £180,000.

He came and spent the summer months on the island, enjoying the solitude before returning back to his winter residence in the Bahamas. This is where Bernie had met him whilst on holiday. Barnes had been a big fan of the band back in the day. Bernie had received an invite to one of Barnes' exclusive cocktail party in Nassau, the capital, at the Ocean Club, the 5-star Four Seasons resort. Both men got on like a house on fire, being around the same age and both children of the 50s.

When Ricky and Bernie had got together and talked about the possibility of recording some new songs, Bernie had automatically thought of Barnes' house. The house was named *An Diadan*. Translated, it meant "haven" or "shelter".

The property, thanks to Barnes, had had a huge makeover. It now sported an indoor gym, swimming pool, cinema, huge wine cellar and a state-of-the-art recording studio where it was regularly hired out to bands or solo artists to record. It took three years to renovate to the specifications Barnes wanted. The location was remote and quiet; a perfect place to reflect, write and record.

To get to the island, the band and recording crew would now have to board a ferry boat. There was a docking pier on Ruma but only exclusively for Harvey Barnes' boats and guests. The island was totally off limits to the public. To meet the boat, they needed to get to the ferry terminal, which was at a place called Berneray, a 45-minute coach ride away.

All the band's instruments and the sound and recording crew's equipment had been brought to the island a few days ago, so, apart from a few suitcases, nothing much had to be loaded onto the waiting coach. The time was 6pm. If all went to plan, they would be at the ferry terminal just before 7pm. The boat journey would take roughly over an hour, weather and currents permitting.

On the bus were the band. Ricky Wilder, Marshall Meyers, Rory Doyle, Erik Olsen and Ray Hawkins. The mark 2 originals. Manager, Bernie Garvey, and his personal assistant, Kenny Holton. Next was producer, Brody Willis, and co-producer, Aadesh Singh. Then engineer, Jerry Fuller, and co-engineers, Kerry Piper and Jude Green. That was 12 in all to make the trip.

Harvey Barnes' PA and manager of An Diadan, Sydney Rose, would be waiting at the house to see to all their arrangements and needs. Barnes had also flown in and employed a house chef, catering, waiting staff and cleaners.

The 12 would live in luxurious and sumptuous surroundings in complete privacy on the island for a month to lay down the album tracks. The final mixing and finishing touches would be done back in London. The weather at present may not have been up to much but once inside the house, it was 5-star luxury all the way.

Bernie had also decided the location would keep the band's concentration and not give them too many distractions to take their mind off writing and recording. No mobile phones and no electronic devices. No Facebook, Instagram or Google. Back to basics. It would be a refreshing change for everybody. Yes, there had been moans and groans from all assembled when the plan had been announced, as, in this day and age, not having a mobile phone or tablet available to use was like losing an arm. Bernie had told them a phone or Wi-Fi signal were nearly non-existent on Ruma so they were welcome to bring phones, but there was little chance of them working.

For all his money and fame, Bernie had come from humble beginnings. A house with a coal fire in the grate, outdoor toilet that froze over in the winter. If you wanted to make a phone call, you went down the road armed with a fistful of ten pence pieces to find a phone box with a phone that had not been vandalised and still worked. So, the band's protests fell on deaf ears. No, he was convinced this was the method needed to produce a great album in the shortest time possible.

He recalled reading about the heavy metal icons, Black Sabbath, recording their classic 1973 album, *Sabbath Bloody Sabbath*, in Clearwell Castle. The grade

II listed gothic mansion in the Forest of Dean, Gloucestershire, served as the dark inspiration the band were looking for. Rehearsals took place in the castle's dungeon, an area that allegedly gave lead guitarist, Tony Iommi, the inspiration for the riff to title track, "Sabbath Bloody Sabbath". He hoped this house would serve the same purpose and produce a record of that magnitude.

Although Harvey Barnes was a friend, he wasn't giving them the run of his house for free. Everything came with a price and time was money. All the band needed to do now was produce a shit-hot comeback album with some killer tracks. What could be simpler for these wily old pros?

Chapter 6

The boat trip was a little choppy to say the least but Barry the boatman, a genial Captain Birdseye lookalike in his early sixties, expertly handled the vessel and navigated it without incident to the docking bay at the pier.

The time was 8.05pm and the bad weather had seemed to have passed for now. The sky on the journey over to the island had gradually cleared and a watery moon now casted a ghostly glow down onto the pier as everybody exited the boat.

'Thank fuck I am on dry land,' said Ray Hawkins. 'I hate boats. When I was a kid, my old man took me out on a mackerel boat fishing down at Weymouth. A storm came in and the little boat was tossed about on the water as if it was made from cardboard. The waves were coming over the side of the boat and everything. I thought I was going to die that day. Since then, I avoid them like the plague. You are lucky I got on this one, Bernie.'

Bernie smiled. 'Luck didn't come into it, Ray. Visions of a big fat pay cheque and a new Harley Davison no doubt got your hairy ass out here.'

Ray showed Bernie a middle finger salute. The rest of the group broke into laughter.

When it died down Ricky asked, 'So how far is this house then, Bernie?'

Just then a torch beam broke the darkness and a voice said, 'Not far. I will show you the way, everybody.' The voice belonged to a woman who stepped into the view of the pier lights. 'Sorry I am a little late. My name is Sydney Rose. I am Mr Barnes' PA and house manager. Welcome to the island of Ruma. I will be looking after you all during your visit to *An Draden*.'

The assembled group regarded Sydney. She cut a striking figure. Probably in her mid-thirties and standing six-foot-plus, she looked almost Amazonian. Her blonde hair was cut short. She was dressed in a black trouser suit over which she wore a long black leather coat. On her feet she sported a pair of black Dr Marten boots.

As the moon shone overhead Sydney's features were accentuated. Her eyes were icy blue. Her lips were covered in blood-red lipstick. Her beauty was quite breathtaking and had not gone unnoticed by Ricky Wilder and the rest of the band. She reminded Ricky of a young Annie Lennox.

'It is a pleasure to welcome you to the island and I hope your stay will be a good one. I apologise that there are no cars or vehicles allowed on the island but the walk to the house is a short one. The boat you came in on is the only way back to the mainland.' Everybody regarded the retreating boat heading back to the Outer Hebrides. 'Don't worry, folks, Barry will return at a moment's notice if I contact him,' said Sydney as if reading the other's thoughts. 'Mr Barnes insists on complete and utter privacy and we have to respect this. As you may know, he is a very reclusive man these days and insists on total seclusion.'

Rory leaned over close to Erik. 'This guy makes Howard Hughes look like Billy Butlin.'

The big Norwegian grinned and then said, 'Who the fuck is Billy Butlin?'

Rory just shook his head.

Sydney continued, 'There is no landing strip for planes or helipads and drones would have a job to reach here undetected.'

'Sounds more like a prison than a holiday retreat,' remarked Ricky.

Sydney smiled revealing two rows of even white teeth. 'Oh, I assure you all the house will give you all your home comforts and more. Don't worry, you won't have to slop out in the morning or answer a roll call.'

'Well, after that COVID shit and the lockdowns of late I am just glad to be free to do whatever I want. So, I am one happy bunny,' said Erik Olsen.

Everybody laughed. Erik's words had certainly been true. The last couple of years had been unprecedented, and the UK hadn't seen anything like it since the last World War. Each member of the assembled group had suffered some personal misfortune during the pandemic. Being back together and to get this project under way was a godsend for them all. They never imagined in a million years they'd be making another album.

'Now, if you'd like to follow me, I will show you the way. Please watch your footing as the ground is slippery from the rain. Try and stay on the pathway, which is lit, and it will lead straight to the house.' With that, she turned and began walking up the hill. Everybody followed.

The barren landscape stretched for miles. Stone, gorse, and heather were in abundance. The scenery was wild and rugged but also strangely beautiful.

'Now that is one beautiful woman,' remarked Ricky to Marshall.

The younger man grinned. 'Ricky, my man, you are old enough to be her dad.'

Wilder grinned. 'Maybe she likes a father figure.'

Marshall shook his head. 'I would say that lady is off limits.'

Wilder looked ahead at the disappearing figure of Sydney. 'Only time will tell, my friend.'

Producer Brody Willis and the rest of the team led the way behind Sydney. Brody was originally from New York before settling down in London with his British partner, Colin, a tennis pro. Unashamedly gay, Brody was an outspoken character and also a tough one, being brought up in the borough of Manhattan in the Meatpacking District, which was not an area for the faint-hearted. He had been a decent amateur boxer when he was younger before choosing music for a career. He had produced records for some of the biggest artists in the world and was a top man in his field.

'I don't know about you, Aadesh,' he said, glancing towards his co-producer, 'but this looks a godforsaken hole. I just pray this house does a good fillet steak and has a comfortable bed. The sooner we get the band to record, the sooner I can get back to the comfort and familiarity of my Chelsea pad.'

Aadesh Singh was a handsome twenty-something Asian man, half Brody's age. He smiled. 'Brody, has anybody ever told you fame has turned you into a snob?'

Brody smiled back revealing stunning white teeth against his sunbed tan. 'I do hope so, young Aadesh. I do hope so.'

Aadesh had worked with Brody for around five years now, learning the trade from a master, and had become over time his invaluable right-hand man and hopefully, one day, he would become his successor. He was a smart cookie, university educated and a wizard on the mixing decks. They made a good team.

The head engineer, Jerry Fuller, who had celebrated his fiftieth birthday a week ago, was a seasoned pro who had worked with the likes of the Rolling Stones, Foreigner, Bryan Adams and Guns N' Roses, amongst others. As head engineer, he would run the show when it came to recording. He would decide where the microphones would be set up in the recording booth, as well as make sure that everything in the booth was set up for a comfortable playing session for all the musicians. As part of this role, he would also set up all the recording levels, preamp settings, and all the other technical settings. Everything he would do was in service of the main goal: recording the best possible take they could every time.

Jerry was very good at this and was much sought-after. He had just recently finished recording an album with the Red Hot Chili Peppers in California and, after this gig, was heading off to Barbados to record a new album with Sting. He was a no-nonsense, straight-talking Geordie who loved his work and didn't suffer fools. Being around the music scene in one shape or form all his life made him a vastly experienced person to have on board.

Co-engineers, Kerry Piper and Jude Green, were earning their spurs working with Fuller. Both were in their early twenties and an item romantically as well as work colleagues. They both had graduated from

Falmouth University in Cornwall as sound engineers and fell on their feet when they got a job working with the legendary Jerry Fuller. They were both literally living the dream and loving every second. The three of them had all worked with Brody previously.

Making up the group was Bernie's PA, Kenny Holton. He had only been working for Bernie for a few months. They had met at a music awards show in London. He was a smart, 30-something, with decent experience in the advertising business. His credentials were impressive. Bernie thought having him on board would be a bonus for the band's promotional side. He also took care of all day-to-day stuff that Bernie could be no longer be assed to deal with himself.

Kenny Holton was a quietly spoken and reserved man but Bernie knew from his CV that he had served in the British Parachute Regiment when he was younger and had seen action in Kosovo, although Kenny himself never talked about any of his military past. In the short time he had been with Bernie, he was proving to be a tough negotiator. He was rapidly becoming a valuable asset. His army discipline and organisation was a bonus. Kenny's trademark designer glasses collection may have made him look a little nerdy to some but they would be foolish to underestimate him as he was also a black belt in ju-jitsu. Bernie loved this fact and felt safe around him.

The "dream team" put together by Bernie was here with the hope of making and recording a blockbuster album and getting the music of Stormtrooper not just out to their eager and loyal fans but also to a new generation of metal followers. Bernie and the band knew this was their last chance at another shot of fame and would hopefully keep them comfortable in their old age.

The house finally came into view and everybody had to admit it was an impressive, if not foreboding, sight amongst the barren wilderness of the rest of the island.

'Fucking hell, it looks like something out of a Count Dracula movie,' remarked Rory.

'No surprise there, my friend,' answered Erik. 'Harvey Barnes made a number of horror films in his time. He is up there with Romero and Carpenter when it comes to giving the audience a good scare.'

'Never heard of him. Anyway, I am more your James Bond type of guy.'

An Diadan's two circular stone turrets at either end of the building gave it the feel of a Bavarian castle. A huge satellite dish on the outside of one of them was the only giveaway sign that this wasn't just an 19th century dwelling. Ricky counted at least seven large chimney stacks and dozens of beautifully crafted windows. Welcoming light shone from two of the downstairs ones.

There was also one lone light way up high in a small window in the west turret. Ricky momentarily thought he saw a figure looking down from it. He suddenly felt a chill crawl up his spine but when he looked again there was nothing there.

As they drew closer to the house, they could see more detail. A large, sheltered porch with two stone statues that resembled Cerberus, the mythical three-headed dog that guarded the underworld, stood menacingly either side of it on guard. Concealed beyond was a solid oak front door with a brass lion-headed knocker.

Sydney stopped on the steps of the porch and faced the group. 'Here we are and welcome to *An Diadan*, everybody. I hope your stay will be a pleasant one.'

She went up to the front door and inserted a brass key into the lock and the door opened. Ricky expected it to creak on its hinges and for a corpse-like butler to appear to welcome them in. But no. Sydney pushed open the door and invited them all inside. Everybody was grateful to get into the warm after the boat journey.

They all stood in an impressive entrance hallway with a flagstone floor and timber staircase to the left with carved balustrades leading to the next level. Another similar staircase to the right descended downstairs.

'Leave your bags here and I will arrange for them to be brought to your rooms. Now follow me into the drawing room and I will arrange tea, coffee or something stronger whilst the chef prepares supper.'

Everybody dropped their luggage and headed to a room on the left.

The 32-foot drawing room featured an exceptional plasterwork ceiling. A huge inglenook open hearth with a roaring log fire. There was an original polished wooden floor throughout the room with a scattering of expensive looking Persian rugs. The large bay window would provide breathtaking views across the island and the sea beyond in the daylight.

'A drinks cabinet is in the corner; please help yourself,' said Sydney. 'Anybody for tea or coffee?'

Most went for the drinks cabinet, which was in the quirky design of the Norman Bates house on the hill from the classic Hitchcock film, *Psycho*. A humorous sign on the front of the doors read, "Mother says drink responsibly". Everybody headed over to it except Brody Willis, who asked for a cappuccino. He had been dry for 10 years and had conquered his desire for the demon drink which had at one time threatened his burgeoning career.

Aadesh, from the teachings of his Muslim religion, refrained from alcohol. He was also into his health and fitness big time, running ultramarathons in his spare time, so he opted for a green tea.

Sydney told them all to make themselves comfortable and she left the room.

Once drinks had been sorted everybody took seats on the three large sofas and numerous easy chairs dotted around the room. Bernie raised his glass of Irish cream. 'I propose a toast. To the rising of Stormtrooper from the ashes and new success.'

Everybody raised a glass. 'To success.'

Kerry Piper and Jude Green, who were the youngest members of the group, stared in awe around the room. Kerry was a red-haired, green-eyed little bundle of dynamite. Always upbeat and optimistic. Jude had a matt of dirty blonde hair and a deep tan that made him resemble a west coast surfer rather than a sound engineer. He was as enthusiastic as his partner and a fun guy to be around.

Jerry Fuller quietly sipped on his vodka and tonic, mildly amused at the young couple's expressions. He was never a great one for small talk. Everybody he met told him he resembled film actor, George Clooney. This secretly pleased him and he liked to play to the charismatic image.

'OMG, this place must cost a fortune to run. I have never been in anywhere like it before. I feel like royalty,' remarked Jude.

'A bit like Brody over there. He feels like a queen every day,' quipped Rory.

Brody rolled his eyes. 'Fuck off, Rory, you are so 80s. How a dinosaur like you has managed to survive this long evades me, especially with your glaring lack of talent.'

Rory grinned and got up to refill his glass.

Ray Hawkins took a sip of his Jack Daniels on the rocks and let his eyes survey the room. 'I thought Jimmy's place, Bracknell Hall, was a palace but this is a step up. Remember that ridiculous self-portrait he had hanging in the dining room. It was fucking hideous.'

'Our Jimmy did have delusions of grandeur. Bless him,' said Bernie Garvey.

'Whatever happened to Bracknell Hall in the end?' asked Erik.

'I heard it became a health farm – spa – that sort of thing,' replied Ricky.

'Yes, that's right. I believe it's now called "Fountain Spa and Retreat",' confirmed Bernie.

Rory laughed. 'A bit ironic after Jimmy's habits.'

The band became quiet at the memory of Jimmy Parish. It was such a long time ago. Part of Stormtrooper's past. It was some 30 years or more since his passing. Although the band had gone on to huge success, the spectre of Jimmy Parish had hung over them all in one way or another, even after all this time.

Jimmy's body had never been found. It had vanished without a trace. None of them would admit it but they all carried a little bit of guilt inside them. There was a time when they had all been friends and a tight unit. It had been unfortunate that it had all fell apart.

For a moment the room was silent as everybody sipped their drinks in quiet contemplation. The fire crackled in the hearth, sending out a cheery warmth that made the assembled group feel relaxed and thoughtful.

Sydney returned to the room followed by a small middle-aged Asian woman wheeling a trolley with the hot drinks and biscuits laden on it, which she left in the centre of the room and left again without introduction.

'Dinner will be served in 20 minutes. Your luggage has been taken to your rooms and your keys are in the door locks. I will show you to them after we have eaten. As the hour is late, in the morning, after breakfast, I will orientate you all with the house and then you can get on with your work. There is a small number of staff working under me here who you may encounter whilst in the house. Please let them get on with their chores and come to me for anything you may require.'

'Speaking of orientation – I could use the toilet.' It was Kenny Holton asking.

'Of course,' answered Sydney. 'If you go into the hallway and take the descending staircase, you will find the bathrooms on the left-hand side.

'Thank you,' said Kenny getting up out of his seat.

As Kenny headed off to the toilets, Erik shouted, 'I will join you.'

'Me too,' echoed Ray and Rory.

Marshall Myers laughed.

'With all you old boys here and your dodgy prostates, we will never get any recording done.'

'Hey, Marshall, you might be the baby of the band but remember you aren't no spring chicken yourself these days. We all know you dye those blonde locks, sweety,' said Ricky.

'Maybe, buddy. But at least it is all my own hair and I have all my own teeth as well and don't need the little blue pill to enjoy myself just yet.'

Ricky threw a cushion in Marshall's direction. *Twat*, he mouthed.

The general chat and good humour continued.

As the men came back into the drawing room Sydney returned. 'Shall we head to the dining room, everybody, dinner should be just about ready.'

'Great. I am starving. I could eat a scabby horse between two mattresses,' commented Erik.

'By the look of you, you already have, you fat bastard,' replied Rory.

'That's all that fårikål stew and fucking waffles he has been chomping back in Norway,' added Marshall.

'Jævla,' Erik replied as he left the room.

'What did he say?' asked Marshall.

Ricky grinned. 'It was Norwegian, I think.'

'I bet it was a fucking swear word,' mused Marshall.

Bernie smiled to himself as he finished up his drink. It was all friendly banter from the guys and they had missed it. *Here we go again. It's started.* The boys were definitely back in town. A little greyer, stiffer and slower, but he had got them here. Now all that he had to find out was did they still have the collective talent to put together a new multimillion-pound selling album once again? It had been 25 years since the last one and a lot of water had gone under the bridge in that time.

Chapter 7

The supper was welcomed by all assembled. It was a starter of parsnip and coriander soup. The main was rack of lamb and a dessert of raspberry posset. The wines were excellent, coming from Harvey Barnes' own cellar.

Bernie Garvey liked to think of himself as a bit of a wine aficionado. The dry white wine was from France. A Chapoutier Ermitage de l'Oree Blanc. It had an intense taste of toffee and a zing of fruity lemons. Quite delicious. The red wine for the main was a Bordeaux Château Lafite Rothschild, which tasted of chocolate, walnut and cedar. It was a perfect complement to the gorgeous lamb.

'Wonderful dinner, Sydney. be sure to pass on our regards on to the chef,' said Bernie.

Sydney raised a glass in acknowledgement.

'I second that,' agreed Rory. 'I think I could get used to this.'

'I'm sure you could, Rory, but let's not forget why we are here. This record can either be the final hoorah for the band or maybe a stepping stone to a full-blown reincarnation.'

Ricky sipped on his wine. 'I must admit, Bernie, when I called you about the charity gig, I never envisaged us making a comeback album on the strength of it.'

'Are you guys excited by the prospect?' asked Sydney. 'It has been a long time since you were all in the studio together.'

'It has been a while, without a doubt, but I think I speak for the rest of the band that, if we didn't think we had it in us, we wouldn't be here. Sure, the money is going to be handy but we still have a reputation to live up to. We don't just want to make a bit of mediocre music. We want to come back with a record to rival *Into the Storm* or *Riding Shotgun*.'

'What is the new album called? If I may ask,' enquired Sydney.

'You may, my dear,' answered Bernie. It is entitled *In the Dying Light.*

'I look forward to hearing the final product.'

'I promise you a signed copy, Sydney. Hot off the press,' said Ricky.

Sydney smiled and once more raised her glass.

'Well, we have got to make the damn thing first, so let's not get ahead of ourselves, shall we?' commented Bernie.

'Relax, Bernie. You worry too much. We have some great tracks ready to lay down. We are going to smash it out of the park,' said Marshall.

Jerry Fuller now joined the conversation. 'As wonderful as you boys are, let's not forget the production team behind this who are going to make you all sound great, shall we?'

'How could we, Jerry, you are always reminding us about it on a daily basis. I am surprised you didn't walk across the water to the island rather than taking the boat,' retorted Rory.

'Fuck off, Rory. What would a bass player know? You are only in the band to make up the numbers.' It was Brody who chimed in.

The banter between these two men could be vicious. A bread roll went whizzing past Brody's head.

'Bollocks to you too, Brody. All you are good for is twiddling a few knobs, or so your boyfriend told me.'

Bernie knew where this was heading so he stood up. 'OK, guys, let's retire to the drawing room for a night cap, shall we?'

Everybody returned to the drawing room full and satisfied. Sydney stoked the fire and then drew the curtains shutting the night out. She then poured herself a drink. The warm glow of the wall lights and the crackling embers in the hearth once again created a cosy atmosphere.

'So, Sydney, how long have you been working for Harvey Barnes as his PA?' asked Bernie.

Sydney sat on a chair near the fire and sipped her brandy. 'About six months.'

Ricky joined the conversation. 'How did you get the job?'

Sydney paused, mid-sip. 'Well, it is a strange story.'

'Go on,' prompted Ricky.

'I saw on social media that my predecessor had died in a freak swimming accident in the Bahamas. I was a big fan of Harvey Barnes' work and desperate for a job so I contacted his website after a few weeks when they were advertising the position and I got an interview for the job. Harvey came to London to hold the interviews personally. He liked me and gave me the job there and then.'

'Have you been in this line of business long?' asked Bernie.

'No. Not really,' replied Sydney. 'I have been in and out of many jobs, but never found anything I wanted to stick at. I travelled around a lot and never really put down roots. I worked in the hospitality business for a while so I am used to meeting people and looking after them. Maybe that is why I got the job in the end.'

'Taking nothing away from your professional skills but I suspect old Harvey fancied you,' said Ricky.

Sydney smiled. 'No offence taken, Mr Wilder...'

'Ricky, please.'

OK, no offence, Ricky, but I would have suspected this myself but Harvey Barnes is 80 years of age and openly gay.'

Ricky raised his hands. 'I stand corrected. Sorry. Can I ask you – when you took this gig had you heard of the band before?' enquired Ricky.

'Why of course I have heard of you. I follow all genres of music and when it comes to heavy metal, you are right up there. I even own a few of your albums.'

'Favourite song?'

Sydney thought for a moment. 'Tough question. But I like the little known track on the *Stormtrooper* album called "NOTHING IS AS IT SEEMS".'

Ricky raised his eyebrows in surprise. 'Unusual choice. Any particular reason why?'

'It's got a catchy hook and, no offence to you, Ricky, but I think Jimmy Parish's vocal on it is incredible.'

'None taken,' Ricky replied.

Sydney glanced to the dancing flames in the hearth and seemed to drift far away. 'The lyrics suggest you can never really know everything about another person. Even if they are close to you. People can be there for you all your life and then turn on you. It's very sad.'

'You sound like you are speaking from experience,' said Ricky.

Before Sydney could reply somewhere outside there was a noise that sounded like a wild animal.

'What the fuck was that?' asked Rory Doyle.

'There are a small number of feral cats on the island. Nobody really knows how they came to be here. They are a rare breed of wild cats named Sorees. They are about the size of a fox with blonde-coloured fur. They are mostly harmless but can be aggressive in mating season or in protection of their young. One of the former owners probably shipped a few over from the Highlands, I suspect. Sometimes they come into the grounds scavenging for food. If you leave them alone and resist giving them food, they go again. I expect the recent storms have brought them closer to the house,' said Sydney.

Rory nodded. 'I thought for a moment it was the ghost that supposedly haunts this house.'

Sydney smiled. 'Which one, Rory? We have many here. The white lady, green lady, black lady and—'

Ricky suddenly burst into song. '*Lady in red is dancing with me...*'

The room burst into laughter.

Rory raised an eyebrow and looked towards Brody Willis. 'Did you hear that, Brody? This place is full of ghosts. That shouldn't worry you though as you are used to going to bed at night with the willies up you.'

Brody flicked him his middle finger. 'Rory, you are a fucking homophobic bore.'

'What's that, Brody, some sort of gay pig?'

Bernie Garvey cut in on the conversation. 'All right, Rory, that's enough for one day. I guess the phrase "PC" passed you by somehow over the years.'

Rory got up from his chair chuckling to himself and refilled his glass from the cabinet, pouring out a good measure of cognac. 'Well, excuse me, Bernie. Who rattled your cage? The topic of conversation a bit close to home for you, was it?'

'What the fuck does that mean?' asked Bernie.

'He is just winding you up, Bernie,' said Ricky.

Rory took a mouthful of his drink. 'Yeah, like Ricky said, I am just winding you up.'

Bernie became indignant. 'I don't give a fuck about a person's sexuality but just for the record, I have been happily married for 30 years with three children and five grandchildren. I can also assure you, Rory, if I did suddenly decide to bat for the other side you would be perfectly fucking safe.'

Rory laughed and walked off across the room to study what looked like a Claude Monet watercolour on the far wall.

'Well, on that note, gentlemen, I am afraid it is past my bedtime and I need to be up early in the morning, so if you wish, I can show you your rooms before I retire,' said Sydney.

Bernie stood up. 'That would be great, my dear. I think it is about time we all got some sleep. Thank you.' He looked at the others. 'OK, drink up, everybody. It's been a long day.'

'Yes, Dad,' replied Rory sarcastically.

Bernie chose to ignore the comment.

Sydney led everybody up the grand staircase to the first floor. 'The rooms on this level are for the recording crew and also Bernie and Kenny. At the end of the corridor is another staircase which will bring you up to the second level where the band's rooms are located.

Each room has its own bathroom, minibar, coffee and tea-making facilities, 36-inch flat-screen television and king-size bed. The only thing which is very temperamental is the Wi-Fi. It is a right pain in the ass. Sorry.'

'Not to worry on that score, Sydney. It will do the boys good to not be on the web for a while,' said Bernie.

'I don't expect Rory will survive without watching Pornhub,' commented Brody.

Rory said nothing but grabbed his groin suggestively.

Sydney ignored the childish banter. 'Is there anything else you require?' Everybody answered in the negative. 'OK. I bid you all a goodnight and I will see you in the morning. A buffet breakfast will be served in the dining room from 8pm to 10pm.' Sydney turned and walked back down the hallway.

Ricky called out to her, 'So, you don't sleep up here then?'

Sydney glanced back with a small smile playing on her lips. 'No, Ricky. I have my own private quarters elsewhere in the house.' With that, she disappeared down the staircase.

Marshall Meyers whispered in Ricky's ear, 'I told you she was out of your league. She has no interest in an ageing rock star. Even the Wilder charm isn't going to work on that one.'

Ricky didn't reply.

The band and crew wandered off to their rooms. 'See you all for breakfast no later than 9am in the morning, everyone. We have a busy day ahead of us,' said Bernie.

***

Ricky regarded the pale features of Shauna Daly. Her lifeless eyes stared back at him. Her skin was cold and clammy to the touch. He had no doubt in his mind she was dead here in bed next to him.

He was in a shabby bedsit and it was early morning. But where was he? He couldn't remember anything.

His head was fuzzy from booze and drugs. The whole evening's events were a blank. Then he suddenly remembered he was in Dublin, 1979.

He then saw a young Jimmy Parish's anxious face appear at the bottom of the bed. 'What the fuck have you done, Ricky? What have you done?'

Ricky woke with a start.

For a moment he couldn't make out his surroundings, Then as the nightmare receded in his mind, he remembered he was on the island. He threw back the duvet and got out of bed and headed for the bathroom for a pee. This would not be his last visit of the night. That was old age creeping up on him.

Minutes later he returned to the bedroom and walked over to the curtains and pulled them back. The night was still dark. He could just make out a small light of a fishing boat out on the sea.

He regarded the illuminated dial on his Cartier wristwatch. It read 3.15am. The fucking same nightmare again. He went through periods of not having them and then for some inexplicable reason, they would start again. That fateful day way back had continued to haunt him. But some of the details were hazy and lost to him. It had been a tragic accident, he was sure of that, but it didn't make him feel any better.

Jimmy and Ricky had both been so young; only 18 or 19. Their band, TNT, was just taking off and with the money saved from a few gigs, they had both decided to have a long weekend in Dublin. They drove Jimmy's battered old Ford Escort on a Thursday morning, leaving London at 8am and getting to Liverpool at 12.30pm. They then caught the 13.30pm ferry, which took eight hours over to Dublin. They finally found a vacant B & B in an area just a mile outside the city centre called Drumcondra at around 10pm.

The proprietor was a morbidly obese middle-aged woman with the most unappealing blue rinse perm. She was wearing a pair of bifocal glasses that suggested that without them she would be as blind as a bat. She seemed more interested in watching television and eating a huge bowl of jelly and custard than booking them in. She just held out a hand with garish pink nail polish on her chubby fingers and took the money and gave them the keys to their room and front door. No signing in and no rules of the house, which suited Jimmy and Ricky just fine.

They washed and changed and headed to the bright lights of the city to go to the famous Twisted Pepper nightclub. It was the place to be seen and hang out with all the bright young things. This is where they both met Shauna Daly. A vivacious22-year-old redhead born and bred in "Dublin's fair city where the girls are so pretty". Shauna was certainly pretty and she was also a free spirit up for anything. Including wearing no bra, dancing like she was having a seizure, smoking copious amounts of cannabis and taking "poppers", or alkyl nitrite, which came in small vials which you cracked open and inhaled. It was a drug of choice on the club scene in the mid-seventies.

Over the Friday and Saturday, the boys met up with her at the club and they hit it off with their love for music and appetite for drugs. Although she was older than them, the boys impressed her with the fact that they had their own band and hailed from the seductive bright lights of London.

The weekend ended with Jimmy and Ricky going back to Shauna's bedsit, which wasn't exactly five-star. They carried on partying deep into the wee small hours. Then, somehow, tragedy struck. Ricky had woken up in the morning naked in bed with Shauna. He couldn't remember how this had occurred.

That was bad enough but the nightmare was that she was dead. She had choked, it seemed, on one of Ricky's trademark neckerchiefs that had been stuffed in her mouth. This is what Jimmy had told him had happened because his mind was a total blank.

Jimmy said he nipped out at 6am to get some cigarettes and told a confused Ricky later that he had gone out to give Shauna and him a bit of privacy as things were heating up between them. When he had returned, he told Ricky that he had tried to wake them both to ask if they wanted a coffee.

'Both of you were right out of it.' He then noticed Shauna looked a strange colour; something wasn't right. 'I pulled down the sheets and that's when I saw something jammed in her mouth.'

Jimmy felt for a pulse and found none and then Ricky came around and Jimmy asked him what the fuck had happened. Ricky could never remember what had happened in that bedsit but everything pointed to the fact he had killed Shauna mistakenly in some rough sex game gone wrong. But that wasn't like him. Could he have done such a thing in a moment of drug-crazed lust?

Both boys knew if they went to the police to claim accidental death, they were screwed. Two London wide boys over in Dublin in the 70s for a weekend of drinking, taking drugs, and partying. Two long-haired, uni dropouts who played in a rock band. They would be cannon fodder for the no-nonsense Irish police. Two more English wasters to be fed to the hungry mob. This was not an option. So, Jimmy took control.

They cleaned up the place spotlessly and eradicated any sign of either of them being there. They then both slipped out of the flat after Jimmy told Ricky to take the incriminating neckerchief from Shauna's mouth and give it to him. Jimmy said he would dispose of it in the water on the ferry back home. They hoped that whoever found her would presume she died from a drug overdose as her bloodstream was full of them. Luckily, DNA profiling had yet to be discovered until 1984. Any evidence would not be damning if found.

Both boys left Dublin and returned to London. The long journey was done mostly in silence. Nobody in their circle of friends even knew they had been away. They told nobody of their trip. For the next few weeks, they scoured the newspapers but nothing was reported. They were in the clear and they made a pact that it would be a secret between them forever.

Over the coming years, as they morphed into rock stars in Stormtrooper, Ricky always felt Jimmy held that tragic accident over him. His fears became real when Jimmy was offered the book deal. Ricky couldn't have that terrible incident dragged up. Although there was no proof, there was no smoke without fire.

He had phoned Jimmy not long before his death and pleaded with him not to expose the story. He emphasised that if the police took the claims seriously, he would also go down as an accessory. It was then Jimmy dropped the bombshell that he still had the neckerchief and he never did throw it into the water. He had lied. Jimmy had said that it was all the evidence he needed for Ricky to go down. He said he would tell the police that Ricky swore him to secrecy and that he feared for his own life as Ricky had a violent temper. Then he hung up the call. Leaving the sword of Damocles hanging over Ricky's head. He couldn't have his secret exposed now. Not when he had so much going for him. Then, lo and behold, his prayers were answered with the unexpected death of Jimmy. Ricky felt sorrow for his old friend but also an overwhelming sense of relief. Jimmy had knowingly for years kept the incriminating evidence as some sort of sick insurance just in case it was needed. What sort of friend was that? Ricky had lived with the guilt of what had happened all those years ago and he knew he would take that guilt to his grave but at least it was his guilt and his secret alone.

For as long as Ricky could remember, his sleep had been interrupted by the nightmare, but since Jimmy had died, they had somewhat receded. But tonight, for some reason, it had resurfaced, but this time there was something about it niggling in the back of Ricky's mind but he couldn't yet put his finger on what it was. Ricky opened the minibar and unscrewed a miniature bottle of Jack Daniels and drank it down in three gulps and then went back to bed to see if sleep would come.

Somewhere in the early dawn hours whilst he slept, his bedroom door opened and somebody silently entered his room and stood for a while over the bed, watching the sleeping form of Ricky before leaving unnoticed.

Chapter 8

The next morning during the two-hour breakfast window, people filtered in to eat. Ricky noticed Sydney did not join them but just before 10am, she appeared looking amazing in a stunning white trouser suit.

She poured herself a cup of black coffee. 'I trust you all slept well. Now, as promised, I will give you a whistle-stop tour of the house and then I will leave you to get on with your work.'

From the dining room they headed back towards the drawing room and went to the door to the left of it. This opened into an impressive oak-panelled library. It was stacked floor to ceiling with books.

'Christ, I have never seen so many books,' exclaimed Rory.

'I don't believe you have read one either,' chided Brody.

'Here, Brody, read my lips,' Rory mouthed, *Fuck you.*

There also was an impressive gun cabinet holding up to a dozen shotguns and rifles. Ricky let out a low whistle of appreciation. 'Now that is some serious hardware.'

'Do you shoot, Ricky?' asked Sydney.

'I did learn how to handle and shoot a variety of guns for my role in *Above the Law.*'

'Ah, yes. I have yet to catch the show.'

'I shouldn't worry, Sydney, love,' said Marshall. 'You haven't missed anything.'

Everybody laughed.

Ricky walked up to the cabinet. 'If I am not mistaken, that is a pair of Purdy shotguns. Am I right?'

'You do know your guns,' replied Sydney.

At the far end of the library was a robust-looking oak-panelled door. 'What's in there?' asked Erik.

'It's Mr. Barnes' private study and bolthole. It remains locked at all times. There are only two keys to open it. One obviously is in Mr. Barnes' possession and the other I am entrusted with,' answered Sydney.

'Wow, very *Tales of the Unexpected*,' commented Rory. 'I take it we are not going to take a peek in there?'

Sydney's face was stern when she answered. 'You are correct, Rory, and if I did allow it, I would have to kill you.' Everybody laughed uncertainly until Sydney's features broke into a smile. 'Don't look so worried, Rory, I was only kidding. Shall we carry on?' Nobody questioned it further.

Out in the hallway another door led to a large living room. More modest than the drawing room but still fashionable and comfortable. It sported a huge flat-screen television on the wall with a surround sound system.

Next up was what Sydney referred to as Harvey's room of curiosities. It contained a huge collection of horror film posters, props and other memorabilia, as well as objects of witchcraft and occult. The group studied classic horror film posters that adorned every wall, such as, *Dracula, Frankenstein, Curse of the Mummy,* and *The Wolfman.* There were also Hitchcock posters – *The Birds* and *Psycho* – and iconic Italian horror such as *Cannibal Holocaust* and *Cannibal Ferox*. Modern films in the genre, including *Texas Chainsaw Massacre, Friday the 13th* and *The Hills Have Eyes* were also celebrated.

Masks were also aplenty in the room. Clowns, werewolves, Michael Myers and Jason Voorhees, Ghostface. There was also Freddy Krueger's claw. There was an array of prop weapons. Swords, axes, spears, knives and clubs, along with other brutal looking instruments of torture and death. There was half a dozen different suits of armour, from medieval knights of old to the samurai. A couple of glass cabinets contained some weird curios. Many that the group couldn't decipher.

'Is that a fucking two-headed rat in that jar or have I been smoking too much dope?' stated Erik.

'These are items of witchcraft and the occult that Harvey has collected from around the world on his travels.'

'Shit,' exclaimed Rory, 'whatever happened to collecting stamps or cigarette cards?'

'Surely we all have our little quirks and passions. Don't we all have a dark side?' questioned Sydney.

'There is dark and then *dark*, sweetheart,' said Rory.

Finally, there was an area devoted to Harvey's own films.

'I remember watching that film,' said Ray, pointing to a poster for *Blood Lust*. 'Some weird shit that was, man.'

Other posters displayed Harvey's most famous cult films such as *Slaughter Farm* and *Crazy Clown Killers*.

'All this horror film stuff doesn't float my boat, I'm afraid. Give me a good Clint Eastwood film any day,' remarked Jerry.

'What about you, Sydney, are you in to all this stuff?' asked Ricky.

'Yeah. I think it's cool. That was one of the reasons I wanted this job.' Her eyes surveyed the walls. 'This is my all-time favourite Harvey Barnes film.' She pointed to a poster for *Hunt and Kill.*

Everybody regarded the image of a crazed-looking woman holding the severed head of a man in her bloodied hands.

'Call me old-fashioned, dear, but I prefer *Gone with the Wind*,' said Bernie.

'You're just an old romantic at heart, aren't you, Bernie?' quipped Rory.

'Well at least I know a decent film when I see one. I hear your cultural favourite, Rory, is *The Little Mermaid*, isn't it?'

The room burst into laughter again.

'Very funny, Bernie. Mind you don't fracture your funny bone.'

Brody tutted. 'Oh dear, struck a nerve, did we, sweety?'

'Bollocks, Brody. I take it your favourite film is *Brokeback Mountain.*

Brody rolled his eyes. 'Totally predictable, Rory, and also boring.

Sydney checked her watch. 'Time to move on, I think.' Sydney ushered them out of the room.

'That place gave me the creeps,' whispered Kerry.

Jude smiled and put a protective arm around her. 'You are safe with me, babe.'

Kerry rolled her eyes and smiled. 'Yeah, all right. I'll believe you.'

Jude playfully patted her behind. 'Honest.'

Across the hallway and through the dining room was a long corridor which eventually entered into an expansive kitchen where the staff were busy washing and clearing up dishes. A chef, who sounded French, was barking orders out to others who were cutting and preparing food.

'The hub of the house where all the delicious food is prepared,' said Sydney.

Everybody took in the sights and smells of the recipes being concocted before heading back to the hallway and then taking the staircase downstairs. The staircase spiralled around to the ground floor where the bathrooms were situated. Walking past them, they came to two large double doors, which opened out to reveal another long corridor. At the first left they found a home cinema that seated 50 people.

'Mr Barnes certainly knows how to live,' commented Ricky.

Sydney smiled. 'As I told you last night, this house has all the comforts you could ever want.'

Next door was an American-style games room and well-stocked bar. This brought murmurs of approval from many of the assembled group. Further down the corridor was another set of double doors, which opened into a fully equipped gym, and beyond was a large kidney-shaped indoor swimming pool leading onto a spa area. Kerry and Jude were like two kids in a sweet shop. Aadesh was also impressed.

'Will we be able to use these facilities?' asked Jude.

'Of course,' Sydney answered.

Another staircase beyond the spa brought them down to a vast wine cellar. Bernie was suitably impressed. 'God, what a place. I think I have died and gone to heaven. This is a lifetime's collection, I'm sure.'

'Indeed,' replied Sydney. 'Wine is one of Mr Barnes' passions. He will bid at auctions all over the world to get the best vintages out there.

'How much is this one?' asked Ray, pointing to a random bottle lying in a rack.

Sydney walked up to it and studied the label. 'This is a Romanée-Conti Grand Cru 1999. It cost Mr Barnes over £40,000.

Ray let out a low whistle. 'There was I thinking I was a big shot going into my local Sainsbury's and buying a £20 Burgundy.'

Everybody laughed. The sound echoed off the cavernous walls and sounded strangely spooky.

'Now let me show you the recording studio where you will be working.'

They went down another set of short steps right into the very bowels of the house and there stood the studio, complete with stone walls for great acoustics.

'Way back, this room would have been used to store dried goods such as tea, coffee, barley, wheat; that sort of thing. The temperature would have been ideal,' commented Sydney. They all managed to fit inside the walls of the studio to take a quick look. 'Of course, its purpose now is for something completely different,' she continued. 'There is a small but exclusive list of bands and artists that have recorded here in the past. Bowie, UFO, Roxy Music, Aerosmith and Eric Clapton, to name but a few.'

'Now the mighty Stormtrooper will grace this studio to produce a masterpiece,' said Marshall.

'We live in hope, Marshall,' said Bernie.

Jerry and Brody cast experienced eyes around the room. 'This looks excellent,' commented Jerry.

Brody nodded in agreement. 'State of the art. It will be a pleasure to work in here.' There were murmurs of agreement around the room.

They now headed back upstairs and outside. The house looked even more impressive in the daylight. The sky was the colour of grey slate and a light drizzle was falling. There was a smell of sea salt in the air and you could hear the distant crashing of waves. The solemn cries of seagulls drifted in on the keen breeze.

There was a large rustic outdoor barbecue area with beautiful hand-carved wooden tables and chairs fashioned out of tree stumps. There was even an intricately carved totem pole. Again, Harvey Barnes' black humour lingered in the way of a sign hanging from a tree saying "Camp Crystal", in a nod to the *Friday the 13th* horror film franchise.

A 12-hole manmade putting green was visible beyond that and a clay pigeon shooting range. Also, there was an outdoor heated swimming pool which was covered over at present.

'That's about it, folks,' said Sydney.

'I think Harvey Barnes has just about covered all bases in the way of luxury and recreation. Maybe I was too previous with the prison quip,' commented Ricky.

'I understand your concerns, Ricky. As self-contained as it is, many people would not be able to stomach the complete isolation the island brings, especially at night,' replied Sydney. Even with all the creature comforts sometimes it can be a lonely and eerie place.'

'How do you handle it, Sydney?'

'I am a pretty solitary person, Ricky. I handle it just fine.'

Ricky detected in her voice a slight tinge of sadness. He wondered what the story was behind her cool and professional exterior.

Sydney now led them to the end of the front lawns. They looked out across the expanse of the island. 'If you want to stroll outside, you will find many relics dotted around the island from a bygone past. There is even a small stone circle, like a miniature Stonehenge. It was a Neolithic sacred meeting place, so I believe. Over on the far side of the island, by the cliffs, are a colony of nesting puffins. I ask, if you can, please steer clear of them and let them have their space. Also be careful around the cliffs as there is a fair bit of erosion, we don't want to lose anybody to the sea. 'There are also a few small stone buildings dotted about containing maintenance equipment but nothing more. There is no dangerous wildlife on the island but, as I said, just be wary of the cats; they are not in any way domesticated and will bite or claw you if you attempt to pet them or go near their young. Also resist feeding them as they must retain their wildness to survive on the island. OK, I will leave you to it.

'In the recording studio there are facilities for tea, coffee, and snacks. A light lunch will be served in the dining room at 1pm but if you are busy and don't want to attend, it is no problem. Sandwiches can be arranged. Just phone through on extension 1. There are two wall phones in the studio and others dotted around the house. You will be able to reach me on them.'

They all went back inside.

Before Sydney departed, she announced, 'Just to let you know the weather forecast for the coming week is not a good one. Storms are predicted with high winds and torrential rain. It can get pretty rough on the island but, rest assured, we have plenty of supplies and our own generator system if the power goes down, which unfortunately it does from time to time in severe bad weather. Many parts of the house are on different electrical systems so it can be unpredictable exactly what power will work and what will not. It can be a bit of a lottery. All of your rooms do have flashlights and there are a number of torches in the hallway cabinets. If you need anything further, remember to dial extension 1 on the numerous house phones.' Sydney disappeared in the direction of the kitchens.

'Right, guys,' said Bernie, 'Let's head down to the studio and do some work. Oh, Kenny, is the meeting with the record company still on in Glasgow the day after tomorrow?'

Kenny Holton looked up from inspecting a beautiful René Lalique vase that sat on a small occasional table. Kenny had a passing interest in antiques and suspected this piece cost a small fortune. He had wanted to pick it up and take a closer look but now decided against it. He answered Bernie.

'Yes, I confirmed it all on the plane over, Bernie. Leave it with me. When the time comes, I will organise the ferry back over from the island and then the plane is scheduled to take me back down to Glasgow. I will stay overnight and then come back here. Barry the boatman will radio Sydney to let her know my travel plans and arrival times.'

Bernie smiled. 'Good man, Kenny.'

'I have paperwork to catch up on so I will be in my room if you need me,' added Kenny.

Bernie watched him go and then turned to the rest of the group. 'Right, let's go make a record.'

Once everybody was set up in the recording studio and in their places, Jerry Fuller took over the proceedings. The band's new album was to be entitled *In the Dying Light*. Ricky Wilder had written most of the tracks and Marshall Meyers had co-written two. The first planned single from the band, "STAND UP AND BE COUNTED", was a full-on rocker with a stadium anthem. This was going to be the first track recorded as a single and the opener on side one of the album.

Brody and Aadesh went into the control room and sat at the audio mixing consoles, ready to work their magic. Jerry would oversee the production process. Ricky was in the studio to record the vocal whilst the rest of the band were in isolation booths to accommodate their instruments, amps, and speakers. The isolation booths helped stop the sounds of their instruments being audible to the microphones recording the singing voice. They would join Ricky in the studio to do the harmonies later. The team would, piece by piece, bring it all together to make the song.

Bernie watched on with anticipation. No matter how many times he was in a recording studio, it never failed to excite and fascinate him as the process of making a record started and began to come together. It reminded him of a top chef preparing the separate ingredients for a culinary masterpiece and then bringing it all together to present the finished dish.

Ricky started his vocal and Bernie smiled. The voice was still 24-carat gold. He hadn't lost any of the gravel and grit which characterised the band's sound after Jimmy Parish. He had been against Ricky taking over the vocals when there was talk of getting rid of Jimmy but now he realised it had been the right thing to do for the band. Ricky had proved to be a more than worthy successor.

Since the band broke up, Ricky had received the most success individually in the music world and, later, television. The three solo albums he had produced had all been successful, with Ricky exploring a more bluesy and soulful type of sound. Marshall Meyers and Ricky, under the name of Double Trouble, had also scored a number one hit some years back with a cover of Phil Lynott and Gary Moore's "Out In the Fields". They had planned to follow this up but Ricky's offer of television work in the States had put this on hold.

Marshall Meyers now struck up his Gibson Les Paul. His blistering guitar work was second to none. Bernie had seen and heard the best rock guitarists in the world, from Hendrix, Beck, Clapton, Gallagher, Page and Blackmore to Eddie Van Halen, Slash and Angus Young, and he felt Marshall was right up there in that iconic league.

Ray 'Hammer' Hawkins played the drums as if his life depended on it and his thumping beat played through all the band's biggest songs. Ray had, five years ago, been involved in a horrific car accident on the M25 when his car smashed into the back of a lorry that had suddenly been forced to do an emergency stop when, freakishly, a cow randomly wandered onto the motorway from a nearby farm. Ray sustained a skull fracture, four broken ribs, a fractured right femur bone in his leg and also a broken left wrist. He was lucky to be alive. He spent a long time in hospital before endless months of physiotherapy. Nobody knew, as he made his recovery, whether he would drum again. But the man was a fighter and a tough cookie. His sunshine lifestyle in California had helped ease the aches and pains of his body and here he was banging out a beat like nothing had ever happened to him. The noticeable limp from his right leg was the only outward sign of the accident.

Rory Doyle was the bassist. Born and bred in Belfast, Northern Ireland, he grew up in a Catholic family amongst The Troubles, living on the fringes of the Falls Road. He was a tough cookie but also had a keen sense of humour, not always shared by the other band members. He was the joker in the pack.

Erik Olsen was the keyboard wizard born in Norway. His nickname was the Viking. He had a mane of startling blonde hair, even if, these days, the colour came out of a bottle. He was adorned head to toe in a vast array of exotic tattoos. When Bernie first recruited him into the band, he had commented of Erik that Shakespeare had used less ink writing his 37 plays. Erik and Rory keep things tight and organised whilst not being spectacular. Both brought essential elements to the overall sound of the band.

As the tracks began to be laid down it sounded like the band had never been away from the studio. Time doesn't erode experience and quality. The top bands in the world seemed to just have a natural chemistry to gel together almost instantly whenever they played. No matter how long it had been since they last met up. The Rolling Stones had this knack and so did Stormtrooper. The band may have been older but the craft and the musicianship was still evident in their performing.

They worked through lunch ordering sandwiches into the studio. By 5pm, three tracks were done.

"Stand up and be counted", "Hunting Love", and "Dark is the Night". Everybody was happy with their work and headed to the games room for pre-dinner cocktails. Kenny Holton joined them and everybody was in a jovial mood.

The games room was modelled on a 50s style American bar/diner. Harvey Barnes had named it *Tony's Place* after his late partner whom he lost to cancer some ten years ago. *Tony's* was not just designed as a memorial to Harvey's partner but also as a celebration of all things vintage America, which they had both loved. It had two blue baize pool tables, half a dozen pinball machines, a couple of old school one-armed bandits, three card tables and a vintage 1950 Wurlitzer model jukebox in the corner. The only break from the 1950s theme was four retro gaming machines; *Space Invaders, Pac Man, Defender,* and *Street Fighter.* The bar was a good 20-foot long. The polished wood surface was spotless. It was fully stocked with every kind of drink imaginable. It also had four working pumps with two American taps, Budweiser and Coors, and two British ones, Bass Export and Blackthorn Cider.

'What a place this is,' remarked Ray Hawkins as he studied the array of framed photographs adorning the walls of classic Hollywood film stars, from Cagney, Edward G Robinson and Betty Davis, to Bogart, James Dean, Marlon Brando and Marilyn Monroe.

'My idea of paradise,' replied Rory Doyle as he headed behind the bar. 'What will it be, everybody?'

Drinks were ordered and they all chilled out. Ricky and Marshall made a beeline to a pool table whilst Brody and Aadesh took the other. The rest played on the machines or sat chatting. Bernie sipped on his

Baileys and fired up the jukebox which contained some classic tunes through the ages, including "New York, New York" by Sinatra, "Always on my Mind" by Presley, "Nights in White Satin by The Moody Blues and "Brown Sugar" by The Stones.

Sydney Rose appeared in the room. She had changed from her trademark white clothes into a red tracksuit with white trim. 'Good evening, everyone. I take it that you had a successful day?'

'A promising start, my dear. A very promising start,' said Bernie.

Rory Doyle, who was back behind the bar, shouted over to Sydney, 'What can I get you to drink, sweetheart?'

'How are you at cocktails?'

Rory grinned and looked in the direction of Brody. 'If you want those type of stories, you better ask him.'

Sydney rolled her eyes. 'Can you make a mojito?'

Rory looked to the ceiling and put a finger to his lips as if in deep thought. 'White rum, sugar, lime juice, soda water and mint. Correct?'

'Perfect, Rory. Thank you,' replied Sydney.

A few moments later, Rory brought the drink over to Sydney who was now sat at a table with Bernie. 'There you go, Madame,' said Rory in his best upper crust English voice.

Sydney raised her glass to him and took a sip. 'Mm. Excellent barman.'

Rory grinned. 'I spent my youthful days working as a barman in the Dirty Onion in Belfast. I have never forgotten how to mix a drink.'

Sydney laughed. 'The where?'

'The world-famous Irish pub, of course. The Dirty Onion is Belfast's oldest building. Dating back to 1780, the building was used as a bonded spirit warehouse from 1921. Known for its Jameson Whiskey and live music. I saw Rory Gallagher play there once. What a fucking legend. You must visit it sometime, Sydney.'

'Maybe I will, Rory. Thank you.'

Rory smiled his infectious smile. 'What's that you say, my lady? Have one yourself? Well, I don't mind if I do.' Rory walked off back to the bar.

'So, Bernie, how long have you worked with the band?' asked Sydney.

'Well, I discovered them in the late 70s and was with them all the way through to the break up. So, it must be 20 years or so. Now it's been six months since they reformed.'

'So, you must know them all so well as you go all the way back to the original line-up.'

'Yes, I have been there for mark 1 and the current mark 2, after Jimmy Parish left the group.'

Sydney took a sip of her cocktail. 'My understanding was that Parish got the sack rather than left?'

Bernie coughed awkwardly. 'Yes, he was sacked. That is true.'

'That must have been a tough decision. After all, Parish the poster boy, lead singer and main songwriter, wasn't he?'

Bernie looked solemn for a moment. 'Yes, it was one of the toughest things I ever had to do.'

Sydney nodded. 'I can imagine. Whose decision was it to get rid of him?'

Bernie looked around the room. 'It was a collective decision between the band and me. Our American record label was also keen to get rid of him as he had become a liability. The rest of the boys in the band just didn't know what Jimmy was going to do next. The booze and drugs were taking precedence over the singing and writing. So we all had a meeting and decided Jimmy's fate.'

'Did you have the casting vote?' asked Sydney.

'Yes,' replied Bernie. 'Ricky and I ultimately broke the news to him.'

'How did he take that?'

Bernie smiled ruefully. 'Not well at all. It crushed him, to be honest.'

'Did you feel guilty?'

Bernie stared into space. 'Yes and no. Jimmy Parish could be a nasty piece of work if he wanted. He was threatening all sorts against the band.'

'Like what?'

Bernie squirmed uncomfortably in his seat. 'Well, let's say, as a rock band in the 80s, Stormtrooper weren't exactly choirboys. It's not important now. Water under the bridge. Things move on. The band has moved on.'

Sydney took another sip of the mojito. 'How do you think Jimmy Parish died?'

Bernie looked at Sydney. 'I have no idea.'

'Any theories?'

Bernie smiled again. 'Oh, dozens, dear, but none can be proved.'

'Do you think his death was a result of him being kicked out the band?' quizzed Sydney.

'His death was some while after he left the band. I don't think it was connected.' Bernie drained his glass. He then pushed his chair back. 'I am off to the bar. Do you want another?'

Sydney shook her head. 'Not just now.'

As Bernie walked off, Sydney surveyed the room and the rest of the band, her eyes taking in everything.

That evening, the dinner was a good-humoured affair as the wine flowed and the delicious meal of sea bass went down a treat. Bernie regaled the others with anecdotes about his meetings with Deep Purple, Led Zeppelin and Van Morrison, and his infamous drinking session with two legendary wild men, British film star, Oliver Reed, and The Who drummer, Keith Moon, on the set of filming the band's rock opera, *Tommy*. He told them that, after the session, he lost two whole days of his life. Forgotten forever. He recalled also being in the crowd to see Hendrix on the 31st August 1970 at the famous Isle of Wight festival. This was to be his last performance in England. Three weeks later he was dead.

'Another major talent destroyed by drugs,' remarked Aadesh.

'Very true, young man, but that was the nature of rock 'n' roll in those days. I am not saying it's right or condone it, but that was the scene back then. Drugs and booze went hand in hand with the music. Not so much now; it is all mineral water, energy drinks and yoga. Times change and artists are more health-conscious. The extreme excesses have seemed to have died out. Oasis thought at one time they were the bad boys of rock 'n' roll but they wouldn't have held a candle to the heavy metal bands of yesteryear. Boys versus men. Bon Scott, Lemmy or Phil Lynott would have left them in their wake.'

Rory Doyle, who was well on his way to being pissed, shouted out. 'Come on then, let's go around the table. Music stars who died of drugs or drink abuse.'

Bernie looked pained. 'Really, Rory? Have we got to?'

Rory ignored him. 'I will start. Janis Joplin.'

'Keith Moon,' said Ricky.

'Sid Vicious,' answered Ray.

Erik was up next. 'Bon Scott.'

'Dee Dee Ramone,' Marshall came in with.

Rory looked at Brody. Brody took a sip of mineral water and then said, 'Phil Lynott.'

Kerry Piper answered with Amy Winehouse and Jude Green followed with Prince.

Sydney was next. 'I am no expert but how about Bobbie Hatfield,one half of the Righteous brothers I believe ?'

'Good call,' replied Ricky.

'Aadesh, come on, my man, who have you got?' asked Rory.

'Michael Jackson.'

'Yes, Aadesh,' Rory enthused. 'Well now, Bernie has already named Hendrix so it just looks like you, Jerry. Can you complete the full house?'

Jerry Fuller dabbed his mouth with a napkin and looked around the group. 'Jimmy Parish,' he answered.

The room went silent for a moment. 'That was never proven, Jerry, I don't think that counts,' said Rory.

Jerry, who usually had very little to say, pushed the matter. 'I believe Jimmy fell over the side of his boat due to being out of his skull on coke and booze. That is my theory.'

'As you say, Jerry. It's just a theory,' replied Ricky. 'Plus, if that was the case, he would have died from drowning, wouldn't he?'

Jerry laughed. 'That's known as a technicality, I think.'

'Well, whatever, that brings our little party game to an end,' said Bernie.

'Yeah, plus what the fuck do you know about it anyway, Jerry?' slurred Rory.

'Because, Rory, I was at the party on the boat that night. Did you know that?'

The room fell silent. Eventually Bernie spoke. 'I didn't realise. Why not mention this before?'

'Why?' said Jerry. 'It was years ago. I was invited as a guest of the then famous record producer, Christian Bell. I was working for him at the time. Foot on the first rung of the ladder, so to speak. I was just a boy, really, and in awe to be in the presence of Jimmy. In those days, unfortunately, I also had a love affair with cocaine. I was out of it by the end of that night but before I crashed, I spoke briefly with Jimmy in the boat's living quarters. I probably made a complete dick out of myself fawning over him. After a few moments of conversation, he said he was going up on deck for a final nightcap. I watched him drop another line of coke and then half-fill a glass with Jack Daniels before wandering off unsteadily upstairs. My guess is he sat on the edge of the boat to drink it and fell in.'

'Wouldn't you have heard a splash or a call for help?' asked Ricky.

Jerry regarded him. 'If I was clean as I am these days then, yes, I probably would have but as soon as he walked off, I collapsed on the sofa with some girl I met there and that is all I remember until the next morning. I blacked out. I was a young and foolish lad back then. I couldn't believe I got invited to the party. I was in complete reverence of everything and everybody, so much so that I got wasted on free coke and booze in record time.' Jerry looked around the room with a twinkle in his eyes. 'Of course, now I realise most of you so-called rock stars are complete wankers.' He took a sip of his drink as he took a barrage of friendly abuse from the band. Jerry then became serious once more. 'I do feel somewhat guilty that I was the last person to see him alive and I couldn't help him.'

'Maybe he didn't want help. Maybe he jumped in the sea himself,' said Brody. After all, he was pretty cut up about being thrown out of the band.'

'Hey, Brody. He was not just thrown out of the band. It was a collective decision for the better,' retorted Ricky.

Brody held up his hands. 'OK, Ricky. I am just saying. I heard he had financial problems, that's all.'

'Jesus Christ, Brody. He had recently signed a major book deal that would have solved any financial problem he may have had so why would he commit suicide?'

'OK, OK, I was just expressing my opinion.'

'Well keep it to yourself. You know fuck all about it,' fumed Ricky.

Things were becoming rather heated. 'All right, everybody, let's cool it. This is all water under the bridge now,' said Bernie.

Sydney spoke up. 'Jerry, are you sure you were the last person to see Jimmy alive?'

'Well up to that moment, anyway, but I can't vouch for after I crashed.'

'Maybe, just maybe, there could have been somebody else up on deck you didn't know about. Have you ever considered that?'

Jerry regarded Sydney. 'Well, if there was then surely, they would have seen what happened and sounded the alarm or thrown a life belt into the water.'

Sydney looked around the table. 'Not if they pushed him in the water.'

The question hung in the air unanswered. Finally, Bernie spoke. 'A leading question, dear. But the police found no evidence of this. I can't think of anybody who would want to do such a thing.'

'I personally rule suicide out as there was no note, as far as I know. Usually there is a note,' replied Jerry.

'Usually, but not always,' said Rory. 'Anyway, Sydney, you seem to know a lot about the circumstances of Jimmy's death.'

'Any good PA would study the background of their clients; there is a shedload of stuff on the internet, plus as I mentioned, I am a fan.

'Of course,' replied Rory.

'Anyway, we can speculate all night, but there is no evidence to support any theory of what happened to Jimmy,' said Ricky. His death went down in rock history and will always be part of it, just like Buddy Holly or Eddie Cochrane. Another talent taken away too soon. I think the little parlour game has dredged up a few memories now best forgotten. It was a long time ago. I think we should be concentrating on the here and now and the future.'

'Here, here,' said Rory. 'Let's all drink to that.'

The evening had turned a bit flat after the later conversation and gradually people split off. Some went back into the bar and others headed for the drawing room. Kerry and Jude opted for an early night which was greeted by wolf whistles from Rory Doyle and Marshall Meyers. Ricky and Bernie decided to go outside for a breath of air.

A sea mist had ridden in and the landscape had become obscured by the ghostly entrails of the mists swirling around. 'Well, that was a lively debate,' remarked Bernie.

Ricky stared out into the darkness. 'What is this Sydney's angle? I thought she was a PA to Barnes but she is coming over more like a…'

'A journalist?' finished Bernie.

Ricky regarded the older man. 'You think so?'

She asks a lot of questions but maybe that is just because she is here looking after us and has an interest in the band as well as being a fan.'

'Possibly, but what about the crack about somebody pushing Jimmy into the sea. What is that about? Could she know something we don't?'

'There is nothing to know, Ricky. I suspect Jerry is right. It was just a stupid and needless accident. Let's face it, Jimmy had become a car crash waiting to happen someday.'

'Yeah, you are probably right. Maybe we are getting uptight about nothing. It just seems strange after all this time to be speculating about Jimmy's death. As far as I am concerned it is yesterday's news and it should stay that way. The band became more famous after he left. That would never have happened if he had still been in it.'

'Or, indeed, alive, maybe?' replied Bernie.

Ricky regarded him and nodded. 'Come on, it's cold out here, shall we go inside and get a nightcap?'

Both men walked back into the house.

Out of the fog beyond the porch, Sydney appeared. She crushed out a cigarette she had been smoking on one of the heads of the stone devil dogs and went back inside herself. Harvey Barnes was right when he told her she would find this job exciting and enlightening. Stormtrooper and their past certainly intrigued her more than their future.

Ricky turned the key in the lock of his bedroom door and opened it. He immediately became aware of the smell of cigarette smoke. Nothing to do with him as he had given up the habit 20 years ago or more. No good for the voice. He closed the door, flicked the light switch on and walked across the room to the window and opened it. A blast of icy air came into the room. The fog was beginning to lift and the watery outline of the moon was becoming visible. He looked around the room, which was decorated in a mix of Gothic and modern. It was warm and welcoming.

The evening had ended quietly enough with some of the guys playing cards and others content to have a few nightcaps. He had enjoyed a few brandies in Bernie's company. They had talked about the old days and the many loves of Ricky Wilder. Ricky had never been short of a stunning female on his arm for company. He also had two failed marriages behind him.

The first one to Tracy Anne Gold, an American porn star. They had been married in Las Vegas at the famous Little White Chapel by none other than Elvis Presley, or a lookalike anyway. It had been a volatile relationship from the start. When it was good, it was very good but when it was bad, it was fucking awful. They divorced after a crazy year. Ricky's second marriage was to Louise Scott, a British television weather forecaster. She had been the complete opposite to Tracy and a calming influence, but Ricky's then inability to keep his dick in his pants eventually led to their break-up. In both marriages, the fortunate thing was there had been no children involved to the muddy waters of divorce. Both ladies got a handsome divorce settlement and the obligatory kiss and tell newspaper spread.

Both men also laughed about Ricky's one-time passion, whilst living in LA, for keeping exotic pets, including two white tigers and a crocodile. Bernie, in turn, spoke about his own marriage. In contrast to Ricky, he had been married to Kim for 30 years, with three grown-up children and five grandchildren who doted on him. Wherever Bernie had travelled with his job, every night would find him ringing home for a chat and a catch-up. They had even renewed their wedding vows in the last few years and it made the pages of *Hello!* magazine. This would be the first trip he wouldn't be able to phone home but he would get Kenny Holton to message her as he had to leave the island for a meeting in Glasgow in the coming days.

Bernie then related a few more stories from his extensive repertoire, including playing in an exclusive poker game in Las Vegas at the MGM Grand Hotel, organised by the rock band, Kiss. Also, horse riding in Tucson with Sir Paul McCartney, who had at one time owned a ranch there. Around midnight most people started drifting to their rooms so both men drunk up. Bernie told Ricky recording would start at 10am the following morning. Ricky had bid Bernie goodnight at his door and then headed for his room.

As Ricky turned away from the window, he could still smell cigarette smoke. He then spied its source. There on the coffee table was a cigarette burning down in an ashtray. Ricky raised an eyebrow quizzically. *How the hell did that get there?* He moved to the ashtray and crushed out the offending cigarette, which is when he saw the empty, screwed up packet on the carpet. Ricky picked it up and opened it out, already recognising the brand. Marlboro Lights. He felt a slight shiver run up his spine. They had been Jimmy's favourite brand. He wouldn't smoke anything else. Ricky threw the packet in the waste bin and went to close the window. The room had suddenly become chilled.

As he was shutting it, he glimpsed a light out there in the darkness, somewhere in the gardens. It bobbed around and up and down as if somebody was looking for something. It was too far away for Ricky to see anything else. *Who would want to be wandering around outside at this hour?* He watched the light get smaller until it faded away. It was at that point he heard what he thought was a distant scream. Pressing his face close to the glass, he looked out into the darkness but could see nothing. There was now only silence. Then he remembered Sydney speaking about the wild cats that inhabited the island. *The scream must have belonged to one of them.* He had been unnerved by foxes screaming in the night as a kid when he stayed with his Aunt Rose and Uncle Tom at their farm in Sussex. Many a night he recalled hiding under the blankets, trembling, until Uncle Tom explained what it was.

Ricky drew the curtains and began to undress. As he finally climbed into the king-size bed and switched off the light, he couldn't shake off a feeling of unease. He found sleep difficult to come by as the cigarette and the earlier dinner table discussion had brought memories flooding back of Jimmy Parish. Jimmy had hardly ever been without a Marlboro hanging from his lips, even when he had been on stage. He swore it helped the gasping tone of his vocals.

His thoughts wandered again. Who had left that brand of cigarette in his room? Was it just a coincidence? Also, what about the light outside in the darkness and the scream? Maybe he was just getting paranoid after all the recent talk about Jimmy. Finally, sometime around 3am, Ricky drifted off to sleep but it was riddled with nightmares once again involving Jimmy Parish.

Chapter 9

The band congregated in the recording studio all on time, except Rory Doyle. He also hadn't been at breakfast.

'Where is that lazy bastard?' said Brody Willis.

Erik grinned. 'He drank enough booze to sink a battleship last night. I suspect he is sleeping it off. I knocked on his door on the way down to breakfast but heard nothing.'

Jerry Fuller didn't see the funny side. 'I don't give a fuck what he drank. He is getting paid to do a job and time is money.' He looked at Bernie. 'Go and get the twat up and stick some black coffee inside him. I expect to see him here in 15 minutes time ready to roll.'

Bernie raised a pacifying hand. 'OK, Jerry, chill out, you will give yourself a coronary. I will sort it.'

He walked off out of the studio.

Jerry took a deep breath and regarded the others. 'Right, we can make a start by laying down some vocals, Ricky. Go into the booth and we will do the ballad, "Soul Survivor".

Ricky nodded. A few moments later, his voice sounded mellow and introspective as he turned in another great vocal performance.

'Fucking hell, Ricky. That voice is as good as ever. Time and the arenas have not eroded it,' remarked Jerry. The assembled group all nodded in agreement.

Ricky's vocals had filled many arenas, including Wembley, Hollywood Bowl and the Beijing National stadium. The eighties had been the era of stadium gigs and Stormtrooper had rocked most of them.

'Right, Marshall, we will get you on the acoustic guitar next and then, Erik and Ray, we will do your bit after,' instructed Jerry.

When Bernie hadn't returned within the hour, the band laid down the next track, a cover of Slade's 1973 number one single, "Cum on Feel the Noize". Stormtrooper were big fans of the Black Country rockers who, in the early seventies, achieved 17 consecutive top 20 hits and six number ones, three that went straight in at the top of the charts, including the timeless "Merry Xmas Everybody". The cover was a homage to them. The song was also a great live foot-stomper.

Bernie eventually returned a little later, minus Rory. 'I can't stir him. He must be out like a light. I knocked and knocked but nothing. His door is locked so I am at a loss.'

Jerry cursed under his breath. 'Right, well, we will have to do without him for now. He can make up for it big time tomorrow and he is off the booze tonight and on tonic water.'

The rest of the band got to work. A few hours down the line, "Raining Blood" and "Highway of Hope" completed side one of the album. The tracks were all rough cuts and a lot of work would be needed to polish them but they were down on tape.

'OK, let's take a lunch break. Everybody back by 2.30pm,' announced Bernie.

As everybody made a beeline for the dining room, Erik said he would check on Rory again. Erik and Rory were close mates in the band and had shared many drunken nights of fooling around and hijinks. Their worst stunt was on New Year's Eve, 1990, in London.

Whilst most revellers were seeing the year in by dancing in the fountains of Trafalgar Square, both Rory and Erik decided to jump off London Bridge after an all-day bender. They weren't only lucky that they survived the drop but also that they didn't die of hypothermia in the sub-zero temperatures of the Thames. Luckily, a partying pleasure boat was passing and dragged them both out. Swathed in warm blankets, they saw the rest of the New Year in on board, drinking champagne and signing autographs. Both of them had more lives than a cat.

The Irish blood in Rory made sure he enjoyed a drink or six. That said, he had never let the band down, so it was strange that he hadn't made an appearance this morning.

'Come on, Rory, for fuck's sake. Wake up, man. Half the day is gone and you are in the shit for missing recording.' Erik listened but he heard nothing from Rory's room. He hammered on the door again. 'Get up, you dumb Mick.'

Just then, Sydney Rose appeared on the landing. 'Is everything OK, Erik?'

Erik looked startled as he hadn't heard her walk up. 'Oh. Hello, Sydney,' he replied. 'It's Rory. He has been in bed all day and missed recording. Pissed out of his head, no doubt.'

A look of concern was etched across Sydney's face. 'When did you last see him?'

Erik thought about his for a moment. 'Last night about 12.15pm. I walked up to his room with him, he was pretty wasted. I said goodnight and then walked on to mine.'

Sydney pursed her lips in thought and then said, 'I have a pass key. I can open the door if you want.'

Erik nodded. 'Yeah, that would be great. The sooner I can get him up, the better for all of us.'

'OK. I will go and get it. I will be five minutes.' Sydney walked back down the corridor and descended the stairs.

Erik knocked on the door again but with no reply. He walked along the corridor and studied some of the paintings on the walls. He was no expert but they all looked expensive. He remembered buying himself a Picasso on the advice of a friend in the antiques trade.

The painting was entitled *L'Étreinte*. It depicted two embracing nude lovers and he paid $20,000.. Two years later, he was bored with it and sold it for $30,000.. Not a bad bit of business.

Erik heard footsteps on the stairs and saw Sydney returning with the pass key in her hand. 'Right, here we go,' she said as they walked to the door. She rapped on it sharply. 'Rory, if you can hear me, this is Sydney Rose and I am with Erik. We are a little concerned that you haven't left your room today so could you just reassure us you are all right by coming to the door or I will have to let myself in with a pass key.' They waited a few moments but heard no movement. Sydney inserted the key in the lock. 'OK, Rory, we are coming in.' She turned the key, opening the door.

Both Erik and Sydney stepped into the room. The first thing they noticed were that the curtains were open. As they walked further into the room, they also saw that the bed appeared not to have been slept in.

'Strange,' commented Sydney.

'I will check the bathroom,' said Erik with concern in his voice. With the amount Rory had drunk the previous evening, he was worried that his friend may have slipped and had an accident in the shower. Erik opened the bathroom door but found the room empty. Inwardly he breathed a sigh of relief.

'Maybe he has gone out for some fresh air,' suggested Sydney.

Erik nodded. 'Yeah. Maybe you're right. He definitely isn't in here. But, in my opinion, this room doesn't look like it has been used at all.'

'Did you actually see him go into his room last night?' asked Sydney.

Erik thought for a moment. 'I left him at the door but, to think of it now, no, I didn't see him go in.'

They both left the room and Sydney locked it.

'What are you thinking?' asked Erik.

'That he might have gone outside for a wander and didn't tell anybody,' replied Sydney.

A look of concern spread across Erik's face. 'Shit, you don't think he fell off the cliff top or something. Do you? The state that he was in last night, choosing to wander around in the pitch black on an island he doesn't know is not the thing to be doing.'

'At this point, I don't think there is any cause for alarm. I suggest you get back to your recording and I will send somebody out to have a look for him. He can't be far. There are, as I mentioned, a few outbuildings on the island used for storage of machinery and gardening equipment he could have crashed out in one of them if he got lost.'

'OK. Thanks, Sydney,' replied Erik. They both parted company.

The band ploughed on after lunch, recording another two tracks. The blistering title track, "In the Dying Light", where Marshall Meyers showed why he was still one of the best rock guitarists in the world, and "Lost and Found", a thumping anthem which showcased Ray's thunderous drumming. It would be an instant stadium hit for the crowd to sing along to. The album was coming together nicely and the new material felt fresh but also held some of the old Stormtrooper magic. Bernie and Jerry felt they were onto a winner.

When the band wrapped things up for the day at 4pm, Sydney had announced that there was no sign of Rory. 'Well, he can't just disappear. We are on a remote uninhabited island surrounded by sea,' commented Ricky.

Aadesh now spoke up. 'Could he have called in the island boat and went back across the water?'

'Why the fuck would he do that?' asked Erik.

'Maybe he took the boat and then contacted that crazy girlfriend of his, Bridget, in Glasgow and told her to fly out to Benbecula? You know they are inseparable these days,' pondered Ray.

Ricky considered this; it was the mad sort of thing Rory might do but had he really gone stir-crazy within a couple of days and wanted to leave the island without telling the rest of them?

Sydney interrupted their musings. 'That wouldn't be possible. He would have to do that through me and I wouldn't have authorised it without speaking to Bernie. As a precaution, I contacted Barry Skidmore, the boatman, on the remote off-chance and he tells me he hasn't been back over to the island since he dropped us off. Anyway, as I said, mobile phone signals are practically non-existent.'

'Is there any possibility he could get a signal somewhere and call another boat to come over here?' asked Ricky.

Sydney considered this. 'It is a remote possibility on the far side of the island, as a signal does drop in and out now and again. Even if by some miracle he got a signal to make a call, any boat coming over here must have authorisation and clearance through me.'

'You have reliable means of communication here?' asked Bernie.

'Absolutely,' replied Sydney. 'It's a two-way radio system that I have in the Mission Control that you can call out on.'

'Mission Control. That sounds like something out of Star Trek,' said Ricky.

'It is the name Mr Barnes gives to the nerve centre of the building where all the security is housed,' replied Sydney.

'Where is this Mission Control located?' asked Ricky.

Sydney dismissed the question quickly. 'It is not something that needs to concern you.'

Ricky held up his hands in surrender. 'OK, Sydney. I understand you have your protocols but it still doesn't take away the fact Rory is missing and it just doesn't add up. If he hasn't left the island then where the fuck is he? Does Mission Control have CCTV?'

'It's not needed as only invited guests of Harvey Barnes come to the island, nobody else can get here or have access. He doesn't want to make his guests feel as if they are being spied on.'

'I would like to search the house and grounds myself,' said Ricky. The band echoed his sentiments.

'The weather is meant to turn in nasty soon and the sea mists will make it nigh on impossible to see. It will be too dangerous,' commented Sydney.

'Well, we can't just sit here and do fuck all,' said Ray Hawkins.

Kenny Holton now spoke up. 'I have to go back to the mainland tomorrow and catch a flight back to Glasgow to meet with our record company. Will the boat be able to come over here tomorrow morning?'

Sydney walked to the nearest window and looked out at the darkening skies. 'I will keep an eye on the weather situation and update you later.'

'Thank you,' replied Kenny.

'No disrespect, Kenny, but who gives a fuck about your travel plans when Rory is missing,' said Erik.

'I am only asking, Erik. The band might be the centre of the universe to you but I also have a vital role to play in its success. Keeping the record company sweet with this new recording is one of them.'

'And let's add to the list sticking your brown tongue up Bernie's asshole,' continued Erik.

Kenny walked off shaking his head. 'Fuck you, Erik.'

'Pussy,' Erik mouthed under his breath.

'Ok everybody that's enough,' shouted Bernie.

'Wait a minute,' interrupted Ricky. 'I have just had a thought. Has anybody checked the wine cellar?'

Everybody looked at each other. 'Shit. Good call, Ricky,' replied Erik. 'Let's go check it out.'

'The wine cellar usually stays locked. He wouldn't have been able to access it,' stated Sydney.

'Shall we look anyway just to satisfy ourselves?' replied Ricky.

They all agreed.

Chapter 10

'You stupid fuck, what a state to get in,' said Bernie. 'You had us all worried. We thought you had gone and fell over the cliff's edge and here you are, sat on your ass, hungover.'

'Never mind that,' fumed Jerry Fuller, 'You have missed a day's recording, you irresponsible little turd.'

Everybody was present in the wine cellar.

When Sydney had unlocked the wine cellar, to her surprise, they found Rory down one of the aisles, crashed out on a pile of hessian sacks. The wine cellar was always locked. How had he got in there? Lying empty next to him were two expensive bottles of Burgundy and a corkscrew. Ricky and Erik had roused Rory so that he was now sat upright, swigging on a bottle of mineral water, looking sheepish.

'Sorry, guys, for letting you down. I went on a right bender last night. I got into my room but was wide awake and wired from the earlier recordings so I went for a walk around the house.'

Ricky recalled the light outside the previous evening and asked, 'Did you go outside last night?'

Rory shook his head. 'I headed back down to the games room and bar but found the door locked but, by a stroke of luck, the wine cellar door wasn't.'

Sydney didn't look too pleased. 'Well, it shouldn't have been. That is wine from Mr Barnes' private collection you drank. The wine in the front racks is for guests. I will get to the bottom of who carelessly left the cellar unlocked.'

Rory held up a pacifying hand. 'No sweat, sweetheart. I will pay for the wine and you can replace it.'

Sydney walked over and picked up one of the empty bottles. 'Château Margaux 2010. Very nice.'

Bernie Garvey swallowed hard. He knew this wine well and what it cost.

Sydney continued. 'This is £850 a bottle. So that is £1700, Rory, you owe.'

The grin on Rory's face disappeared as the rest of the group laughed out loud.

'You dummy,' said Marshall Myers.

Rory looked remorseful as he got up from the floor and headed towards the door. 'Fuck you all. I'm hungry. When's dinner being served?'

Ricky cut in. 'What I don't understand is, when you woke up, why didn't you come back upstairs?'

'Because the door was locked again,' replied Rory. 'I banged and shouted but by then you were all recording and, seeing as the studio is soundproofed, you wouldn't have heard anyway. I got pissed off. I drunk some more wine and went back to sleep.' Rory wandered off.

'This isn't over, Rory,' Jerry Fuller called after him. 'Time here is money and you are wasting it.'

Rory raised a middle finger in the air and didn't look back.

Fuller looked towards Bernie. 'You better sort that little shit out or I will swing for him.'

'All right, Jerry. I know Rory can be a bit of a wind-up merchant and a pisshead but he has never done anything like this before.'

Fuller was not to be pacified. 'Yeah, well, I remember a time you said the same about Jimmy Parish and look what happened to him.' Before Bernie could reply, Jerry Fuller walked out of the cellar and headed up the stairs.

Dinner was a rather subdued affair and after everybody had finished many wandered off to the games room, Bernie found Rory in the drawing room. He was sat by the roaring fire with a bottle of brandy and a balloon glass containing a generous measure of French cognac. He seemed lost in his thoughts but looked up as Bernie entered the room. 'I hope you haven't come in here to give me a fucking lecture, Bernie. If you have, you can do one.'

Bernie held up a pacifying hand. 'All right, Rory. I am not here for a lecture.'

Bernie went to the drinks cabinet and helped himself to a Baileys. He walked over to Rory and gestured to the other armchair. 'May I?'

Rory took a sip of brandy. 'Knock yourself out.'

Bernie settled into the chair. 'Look, Rory, as your manager, I have a right to ask what is going on but as a friend, I am concerned. You know how important this album is and that we have a limited time to record it in. What the fuck has got into you?'

Rory stared into the dancing flames of the fire. Bernie sensed he was making some sort of decision. He patiently waited. Rory swallowed the rest of his drink and refilled his glass. 'I am going to tell you something, Bernie, but you have to swear that you will not breath a word of it to the lads or anybody else here, especially that prick, Fuller.'

'OK, Rory. I give you my word.'

Rory leant forward in his seat. 'Before the band got back together again, I had become unwell. I had begun to experience pains in my abdomen but, at first, I just popped some painkillers hoping they would go away. The tablets seemed to keep the pain at bay but then I discovered blood when I had a dump.' Rory took another swallow of his drink.

Bernie began to have a bad feeling about where this conversation was heading.

Rory continued. 'Anyway, at that point, I should have gone to the quacks, but being a "dumb Mick", I ignored it. Things got worse and by the time we had come back from the greatest hits tour, I was in a bad way but I hid it the best I could from the band. I then did see a doctor who referred me straight to a hospital for tests. They came back to inform me I have bowel cancer.'

Bernie had guessed this as a very dear friend of his had passed away a year or so ago from the same thing. 'I am sorry, Rory. I truly am,' he said.

Rory emptied his glass once more. He smiled ruefully. 'Thanks, Bernie. I should have gone to the doctor sooner; the cancer is spreading to the lymph nodes. My five-year survival rate percentage has gone from 63% to 72%. The clock is fucking ticking. Some days I am OK, others are fucking tough. That is where the booze comes in. I should have given it up with the medication I am on but fuck it. I am going to die sooner rather than later, so what the hell. I just want to finish this album and do another tour on the back of it if I can. That is what gets me up every morning. I will keep going until I can't.'

Bernie nodded. 'The lads should really know, especially if your behaviour becomes erratic or out of character. Jerry already has you down as a waste of space and will not hesitate to push to replace you if you don't get your act together.'

Rory leant in close to Bernie. 'Nobody must know until it is absolutely necessary; I don't want anybody's pity. Do you understand, Bernie?'

Bernie had never seen Rory look so serious and intense. 'OK, Rory. I promise.'

'Good. Subject closed,' replied Rory and got to his feet. 'Fancy a game of pool?'

'Sure,' replied Bernie.

As they walked towards the stairs Rory said, 'I just remembered something, Bernie. When I was in the wine cellar and drifting towards sleep, I thought I saw somebody stood in the aisle I was lying in, watching me.'

'Do you know who it was?'

Rory grinned ruefully. 'The state I was in it could have been Father Christmas, the tooth fairy, or Elvis fucking Presley. I couldn't really make them out fully. Weirdly, I thought it was a cowboy. How fucking crazy is that?'

'Why a cowboy?'

Rory looked at Bernie. 'Because of the Stetson hat they were wearing.'

'Could you have been dreaming or hallucinating?' asked Bernie.

Rory thought for a moment. 'No, I am pretty sure somebody was there. Anyway, let's play some pool.'

Bernie suddenly felt an inexplicable feeling of unease as he left the room.

***

'I have arranged for Barry the boatman to pick you up at 9.30pm this evening, Mr Holton. I think it is a sensible decision to leave the island tonight and go to the mainland as the storm isn't due to hit us until after midnight. You will be well on your way by then.'

'Thank you, Sydney. I will just finish packing and then make my way down to the quay,' said Kenny Holton.

He was stood in the dining room with Sydney Rose and Brody Willis as the remnants of dinner were being cleared away. He had been concerned all evening about his meeting tomorrow and the bad weather coming that might prevent him from leaving the island but Sydney, as promised had come to the rescue and organised the boat to come and get him now.

'No problem, Mr Holton. I hope your meeting goes well. Will you be joining us again?'

'I am not sure. That will depend on whether Bernie needs me back. I won't know until after the meeting.'

Brody Willis put down his coffee cup. 'Do you need a hand with anything, Kenny?'

Kenny raised a hand. 'No, you stay where you are. I am fine. I travel light. A bag and my laptop and I am all good, thanks.'

'OK. Have a good trip and think of us all huddled here being battered by Storm Angela, or is it Alice, on its way.'

Sydney laughed. 'Don't worry, Mr Willis, you will be quite safe here, and it's Storm Alec, by the way.'

'I stand corrected.' Brody took a small bow.

The storm, as predicted, hit the island just after midnight. Everybody watched from the sitting room's large panoramic window as the rain lashed the island and the wind bent the trees in the grounds of the house.

'Well, I am glad Kenny got away safely,' said Bernie.

'I agree,' said Jerry Fuller. 'According to Sydney, this storm is here to stay for a while. I suppose the one consolation is we will all know where each other is.'

Behind his back, Rory Doyle again gave him the finger.

'Where are Kerry and Jude?' asked Aadesh.

'They were heading for the swimming pool then hot tub last time I saw them,' said Ricky.

This raised a cheer from the rest of the band.

'Young love. How wonderful. I can barely remember it,' added Ray.

'Speak for yourself, old man,' chided Marshall.

The good mood seemed to be back in the room and the day's earlier events more or less had been forgotten, probably due to the fact that the bar in the games room was being hit hard.

Rory was back to his old self and the cognac had him in a playful mood even though he had been told to stick to tonic water. 'I am off down to the spa to give those two lovebirds a scare. Look what I found.' From behind his back, he produced a mask and pulled it over his face. 'Michael Myers is back.' The mask was a replica of the fictional killer from the *Halloween* films.

'That's a fucking improvement, Rory,' shouted Marshall.

Bernie fussed like an old mother hen. 'You took that from Harvey's private collection. You better put that straight back. It's an original, I suspect. Remember you already owe him for two bottles of wine.'

'Don't sweat it, Bernie, I will return it after I have had a little fun.'

'Well, go easy on them, Rory, and try not to spoil their whole evening. Plus, return the mask, no exceptions.'

Rory gave him a mock salute and left the room. Bernie looked worried.

'Don't worry, Bernie. I will go check on him in a while and make sure he hasn't done anything totally stupid,' said Ricky.

'Thanks. We all need to be up early and on the ball again tomorrow. So, with that in mind, I will bid you goodnight.'

Aadesh, Brody and Jerry all decided to turn in as well. Jerry looked back at Bernie. 'I am holding you personally responsible for that Irish twat. He better be there on time tomorrow.'

'Yes, Jerry. Message received and understood. Now go and get your beauty sleep,' replied Bernie.

The band decided to have one more nightcap. They retired to the sitting room where the wind was howling down the chimney with such force it blew sparks from the fire onto the hearth.

'Fucking hell. It's like the end of the world out there,' said Erik as he pulled the curtains together again. 'My country has its fair share of snow but not the rain and winds that the UK has.'

'It's probably twice as bad here, seeing as this is such a remote hellhole,' commented Marshall. 'Being born and growing up in the Lone Star State of Texas, I can't ever come to terms with the British weather.'

Ricky got up from the sofa and spoke. 'Pour me a Scotch, guys, I am just going to check on Rory and make sure he isn't stretching the boundaries again. I won't be long.'

Ricky walked down the stairs to the lower level of the house. The force of the storm was making the lights flicker. He walked down the corridor and passed the cinema and games room; they were in darkness. He moved on down the corridor to the gym and indoor pool which led to the spa room. He was surprised to find the gym also in darkness. Apart from the occasional howl of the wind, all was quiet. Ricky fumbled for the light switch panel and found it. The whole place was immediately flooded in bright white light. The gym equipment, all black and chrome, stood like silent sentinels. Harvey Barnes had kitted it out with the latest hi-tech, space-age machines.

In the last five years or so, Ricky had become a frequent gym user. The television work he had picked up played to his vanity and he wanted to be in the best shape possible for an ageing man required to do a few action scenes. Up to now, he had avoided Botox but the powers that be at the show, *Above the Law,* were turning the screw for him to have it for the next season. For the moment, he had kept them at bay. Fitness-wise, though, he was enjoying his workouts.

In his younger days when playing with the band, his weight had not been an issue. He had ate very little, saving his calories for the booze. On tour, running around the stage under the glare of the hot lights for two and a half hours every night had kept him fit enough. He had also enjoyed cycling and swimming, particularly when he had lived in LA for a few years when married to Tracey Ann. But time takes its toll on the body, no matter who you are, unless you are Mick Jagger, of course.

He now worked out a lot more with weights and had even done a few workouts with Mark Wahlberg and also Sylvester Stallone. Both were gym rats. But Ricky, being nearer to Stallone's age, couldn't help marvel at what a beast the man still was and an inspiration to the older male.

As he now walked through the gym, on impulse, he jumped up onto the pull-up bar and banged out ten reps. *Not bad for an old un.* Ricky now came out of the gym and opened a door into the pool area. It was a mightily impressive sight. The pool itself was kidney shape. The water was still and a shimmering bright blue under the overhead lights. At one end of the pool was a massive sixty-second clock for timing lengths, at the other was a 12-foot diving platform and a lower wooden springboard. Ricky felt a small tingling of adrenaline in his belly as he regarded it. He wasn't great with heights. He always joked that he could get a nose bleed changing a light bulb.

Even though he was now a competent swimmer, when his nostrils picked up the smell of the chlorine, he was transported back to being an eight-year-old kid at primary school having his first swimming lessons. Ricky had hated the water and hated his nemesis, Mrs Barber, the battleaxe swimming instructor. He could even recall her sarcastic words clear as a bell now. 'Come on, young man, time to get rid of those arm bands and swim properly. Don't be worried if you go under the water and swallow some, there is plenty left in the pool.' *Unfeeling cow.* Even when he did learn to swim properly, she never gave him any praise. One day, she didn't turned up for the class and he learned that she wasn't well and in hospital. Later he found out she had had a stroke. As a kid, you didn't really know what that meant. The only thing Ricky was glad about was the old cow never came back.

Ironically, many years later, at a record signing in London, an attractive blonde lady had told him whilst he signed a copy of their debut album for her that her mum, Anita Barber, had told her many years back that she had taught a young Ricky Wilder from Merrywood Primary School swimming lessons. Ricky had been stuck for words and never told her what he had thought of her mother all those years ago.

Now he came into the spa area. The massive hot tub dominated the centre of the room. It was running as Ricky could hear the bubbling water. From where he stood, he couldn't ascertain if it was occupied or not. The raised lid obscured his view. There was no sign of Kerry or Jude around. Water on the floor, though, plus a couple of discarded wet towels lying on a lounger, suggested that the couple had been here but now gone. There was also an empty bottle of wine and two glasses by the side of the tub.

'Rory, are you here, man?' Ricky's voice sounded loud and echoey. There was no reply except for the whispering noise of the wind somewhere above him. Maybe Rory headed back upstairs after finding nobody here. *But wouldn't we have run into each other on the stairs?* mused Ricky. His gaze then fell then on a small ornate Japanese table. Sitting on it was a glass ashtray with a lone cigarette burning down in it. On closer inspection, he saw it was a Marlboro Light, just like the one he had found in his room the previous evening. He knew that Rory didn't smoke and neither, to his knowledge, did Jude or Kerry.

The whole room suddenly felt very empty and an icy finger of unease ran down Ricky's spine. He walked up closer to the tub and moved around it to get a better view and that's when he saw Rory sat down low in it. The water bubbling up to his chest. The heat, thought Ricky, coming from the water seemed far too extreme for anybody to sit in comfortably. He noted that Rory was still wearing the ridiculous mask he had taken from Harvey Barnes' collection.

'Rory, you dick. Why didn't you answer me? What the fuck are you trying to do, boil yourself like a lobster? Come on, man, time to hit the sack, we have a big day tomorrow and you need to make up for earlier.' No answer or movement came from Rory. The heat from the tub was now overwhelming. Ricky began to be concerned. 'Rory, come on, let's get back upstairs and have one nightcap or Bernie will have your balls in the morning.' Once more, he was answered by silence.

Ricky was now getting pissed off. He made a grab for the mask and pulled it off of Rory's head. He recoiled in horror as he stared into the eyes of his friend. They were rolled back in his head. The whites were bloodshot. Immediately, Ricky was transported back to Dublin and he was staring into the dead eyes of Shauna.

He found himself beginning to hyperventilate. He shook Rory but his body was floppy and unresponsive; he then knew that he was dead. Ricky tried to pull him from the water but he was too slippery and the water far too hot. He lost his grip and Rory sank back down into the tub.

Ricky suddenly felt spooked. He glanced nervously around the room, feeling vulnerable. The wind still howled mournfully outside as if trying to claw its way into the house. He looked back to the tub with a feeling of dread beginning to rise in his stomach. *Fuck, what had happened here?* This couldn't have been an accident, could it? Rory was fully clothed. He would have had to have been out of his tree to do that. Even in a drunken or high state, he didn't think Rory would be stupid enough or reckless enough to just jump in a hot tub at this temperature. He had to get help but he couldn't leave Rory in the tub burning up.

Ricky eventually found the controls and switched the hot tub off and made for the exit. He then heard a noise from the swimming pool. It sounded like somebody jumping or diving into the water. He ran back into the swimming pool area and as he scanned the water, his eyes suddenly saw the bodies. Two of them floating face down in the middle of the pool. It was Kerry Piper and Jude Green. The water around them was slowly turning into a cloudy red. Ricky froze and stared in disbelief. *What the fuck!* This surely was another nightmare that he would suddenly wake from. Panic set in and Ricky felt his heart beating like a hammer inside his chest. Was he dreaming this and would he wake any moment to breathe a sigh of relief? He stood frozen to the spot, wondering what to do. He wanted to move, wanted to help, but his brain wasn't registering things properly.

He recalled that he had once read an article in a magazine about something called normalcy bias. It was the phenomenon of disbelieving one's situation when faced with grave and imminent danger or catastrophe. This resulted in overfocusing on the actual phenomenon instead of taking evasive action; you could find yourself in a state of paralysis. It went on to describe how people involved in the 9/11 tragedy at the Twin Towers in New York had carried on sending emails and making phone calls as if nothing was happening as smoke billowed into the offices and fires broke out. Ricky knew for sure this was what he was now experiencing.

At the very moment he recognised this, all the lights went out and the whole place was plunged into inky darkness.

Chapter 11

'Shit,' cursed Erik as all the lights went out in the drawing room. He had just been pouring himself a drink when it happened and now he had missed his glass and poured brandy onto the expensive-looking rug. 'What's going on?' he asked.

'It's the storm, I suspect,' answered Marshall. 'Sit tight, the lights will come back on soon.'

As their eyes became accustomed to the dark, they could now make out the glowing ambers of the fire and they moved closer to it.

'I thought Sydney said the house had a back-up generator for emergencies?' queried Ray.

'Chill out, man. It might just be the case of a tripped fuse. It will be sorted,' answered Marshall. 'It could be worse, remember when we were about to go on the stage in Dallas – or was it Denver – for that open-air gig back in '91 and there had just been a massive thunder storm and the lightning cut out all the electrics.'

'Fuck, yeah, 60,000 people thought that the gig would be cancelled but the good old electricians and sound guys got it all up and running again within 15 minutes. Legends,' recalled Erik.

'What a gig that was as well. We fucking killed it,' reminisced Ray. The men fell silent for a moment, all reflecting on that moment. 'I thought Ricky and Rory would have been back by now,' said Ray.

Marshall looked around the dark surroundings. 'If the lights have gone out all over the house, I suspect they are waiting it out somewhere as well.'

Ray nodded.

From outside, a distant scream sounded making the three of them jump.

'Holy crap. What was that?' asked Erik.

The three of them laughed nervously.

'One of those fucking feral cats, I bet,' answered Ray.

'Christ, I nearly shit myself,' exclaimed Erik. 'I wish these damned lights would come back on; I am getting spooked.'

'What's the matter? The big, tough Viking frightened of the dark?' chided Marshall.

Erik ignored the comment.

'Talking of being spooked, what is that light moving outside? I can see it through the curtains, asked Ray.

The men looked towards the drapes on the large picture window drawn tight against the storm. There was definitely a light shining outside ,like a torch beam. It was bobbing and moving back and forth. Marshall got up and moved to the window and pulled back the curtains. That was when there was a tap on the glass and a face looked in.

***

Ricky stood stock-still for a moment, his brain struggling to process what he had just seen. He knew he needed to get help right now so he began to gingerly walk forward, his hands stretched out in front of him, feeling his way in the blackness He felt slightly disorientated and he wasn't sure how close he was to the edge of the pool. He had no desire to end up in there, especially with the bodies of Kerry and Jude. *Jesus Christ, what happened to them and poor old Rory? A tragic accident? A stunt gone wrong? If not, had some lunatic broken in and just randomly murdered them? But how the fuck could they get in the house, or onto the island in the first place, for that matter.*

Ricky moved slowly on knowing that the gym door was somewhere close up ahead. Finally, he felt the doorframe and knew he had reached the entrance. He paused a moment, remembering there were two steps up. He then heard the footsteps. They had sounded behind him somewhere in the darkness. Somebody was following him. He stood completely still and strained his ears. All he could hear now was the wind still howling around the building and the thumping of his heart.

Ricky suddenly remembered he had his mobile phone in his pocket. Although reception was non-existent here, he had, out of habit, just been carrying it around with him. He pulled it out and pressed the button. The screen lit up and glowed a ghostly green colour. He noticed his hands were shaking. There was a torch app on the phone and Ricky scrolled to find it. As he did this, he heard the footsteps again. They sounded closer this time. They moved stealthily but Ricky could detect them. He hit the switch on the torch and a powerful beam illuminated from the end on his phone. Instantly he spun around and thrust the phone out into the darkness behind him.

'Who's there?' he asked. His voice sounded hollow and echoey. No reply.

He moved his phone around, trying to pick up any movement. As good as the beam was, the place was too vast for the torch app to illuminate anything substantial. Ricky now turned back and used the torch light to slowly guide him through the gym and out the other side. As he did this, he reached for the light switches and randomly pressed them on and off. Nothing. He glanced back over his shoulder, but could see nothing.

As he came out of the gym, he could hear music. Moving forward, he noticed a glow of light from the cinema. He now detected this was where the sounds were coming from. Maybe somebody had come down to watch a film. He felt relief flood over him as he ran to the door. As he drew closer, he saw the doors to the cinema were wide open and light illuminated the plush red velvet seats that were all empty. Ricky walked inside. He picked up the faint scents of popcorn, beer and furniture polish.

A film played on the large screen. It was Stormtrooper's legendary concert in 1983 at Madison Square Gardens, New York. The film was also a documentary about the band, called *Storming America*. There on the screen, in full technicoloured glory, was Jimmy Parish belting out the band's classic, "Tough Love". How was this playing and why? The whole place was deserted. This situation was getting weirder by the minute. Part of him almost expected the lights to come on and everybody else would be stood there, laughing at his expense. For everything to just have been an elaborate, sick joke. But no. He stole another glance back over his shoulder to the gym and his eyes caught a shadowy figure standing in the doorway watching him. Ricky couldn't make out their features. All he could see was the red glow from the end of a lit cigarette and the outline of a cowboy hat on their head. 'Who the fuck is there? shouted Ricky. The figure silently melted back into the darkness

***

'Sorry I startled you, Marshall,' apologised, Sydney. I had to go outside to check the satellite dish to see if it had come loose in the wind.'

Marshall acted cool. 'No sweat, Sydney. Just didn't expect to see a face staring back at me when I opened the curtains.'

Sydney now stood in the hallway dressed in a black sou'wester that was soaking wet. In her hands was a large flashlight. Marshall, Ray and Erik had all gone into the hall after the shock of seeing Sydney outside the window and had opened the front door to let her in. 'Thanks for getting the door for me, boys. It blew shut with the wind and I stupidly left my keys here on the hall table. I am glad you were still up.'

'Shit, Sydney, I thought you might have a maintenance person to do things like that?' exclaimed Ray.

'Usually there is, Ray. Old Tom McSweeney, who I think came with the house as the resident handyman but he is off sick. He has been convalescing from a really bad bout of COVID, so for now, I have to deal with it.'

'Just to let you know, then, the power has just gone off in here,' said Erik.

'Yes, and the big bear is afraid of the dark,' added Marshall.

'Fuck off, Marshall,' Erik retorted.

Sydney smiled. 'Right, I will go and check the mains electricity box; I expect a fuse has tripped. It is not unusual in these circumstances. If not, I will have to power up the backup generator. It is situated outside in an open shed. There is plenty of diesel to start it and keep it fuelled, so hopefully we can get everything up and running again. If that is the case, I may need a hand with it.'

'No problem, just let us know,' replied Marshall.

'I heard on the radio earlier that we're going to face hurricane-force winds all night and again tomorrow,' said Sydney. We have had bad weather on the island before but not like this. The house is usually pretty self-sustainable. But this is unprecedented. On the back of that information, I took the precaution of sending the remaining staff back home this evening on the boat that Mr Holton took before the weather closed in, otherwise they would have been stranded here at the weekend and unable to see their families. For now, we will have to fend for ourselves.'

'So, whilst this storm rages, we are effectively marooned here?' questioned Erik.

'That unfortunately is one of the downsides of Mr Barnes' passion for peace and isolation,' answered Sydney.

'Why the fuck couldn't Bernie have booked a recording studio in Saint-Tropez or Marbella,' said Ray.

Sydney laughed. 'I will go and get this electric on and hopefully make things a bit more comfortable for you, Ray.'

Suddenly their attention was drawn to running footsteps sounding on the staircase, coming upwards. Moments later a wide-eyed Ricky Wilder appeared at the top. He swung his phone in their direction as Sydney shone her torch towards him. 'Thank God I found you all. Quick. I need your help, something terrible has happened down here,' Ricky gasped.

Chapter 12

'What the hell has happened to you?' asked Marshall.

Ricky ran towards them. His face was deathly white in the torchlight. 'It's Rory, Jude and Kerry.'

'What's that clown, Rory, done now?' asked Erik.

Ricky grabbed Erik's shirt. 'No, you don't understand. They are all dead.'

Erik looked at Ricky's face and detected the fear in his eyes. He then laughed nervously. 'This is a wind up, right?'

Ricky shook his head. 'No. This is for real. They are all dead.'

Everybody exchanged glances of disbelief and shock.

'Has there been some sort of accident?' asked Sydney.

'No. Yes. I mean, shit, I don't know,' replied Ricky. They look like they could have been murdered, as far as I can see. Rory is in the hot tub and the two kids are face down in the swimming pool. I think I saw somebody downstairs in the shadows. I couldn't make out who it was but they followed me and then disappeared when I challenged them. I then ran back up here.'

'Fuck, man. This is some heavy shit you are laying on us, Ricky,' said Ray.

'They are fucking dead, Ray. No bullshit. I think I would have been next in line if I hadn't got back up here.'

Marshall looked at Sydney. 'Do you know anything about this?'

Sydney looked shocked. 'Good God. No.'

'Who else is in this house besides us all?'

'Nobody. As I told you, I sent all the staff home earlier.'

'Are you 100% sure, Sydney?'

'Yes, Marshall. I am positive.'

'Then who the fuck did this to Rory and the kids?

'I have no idea, Marshall. Nothing like this has ever happened on the island.'

'Could somebody get onto the island and hide in the house undetected?'

'Highly unlikely but I suppose anything in theory is possible, but I don't see how. It would be a one in a million chance,' replied Sydney.

Ricky, now a little more composed, spoke. 'There is somebody downstairs. How they got on the island or in the house, at this moment in time, isn't important. What does matter is why kill them? Who the hell would know we were here anyway? As far as I knew, Bernie kept this whole project tightly under wraps.'

'Yeah but the press or the media have their little fucking ways of finding out stuff and leaking it,' replied Erik.

Nobody answered but each of them were thinking over what had just been said.

Sydney finally broke the silence. 'Let me get the power on again ,if there is somebody dangerous lurking downstairs then we are not going hunting them in the dark.'

'Who said anything about hunting them? Let's call the police,' exclaimed Ricky.

She began to walk off. 'OK. I will sort the power out and then I will be right back.'

'Wait,' said Marshall.'I will go with you just in case.'

'Thank you. The fuse boxes are situated in the basement beyond the kitchens. Not the nicest of places to go wandering in the dark,' Sydney replied. Both Marshall and Sydney headed off into the darkness.

Ricky flopped down into an ornate Georgian wingback armchair and related the whole story. Erik and Ray listened wide-eyed at what they were told. As Ricky finished, the lights came back on. The three men blinked momentarily as their eyes got used to the brightness again.

'Who would do such a thing? I don't get it,' said Ray.

Erik shook his head. He had no rational answer. He couldn't believe his friend was gone. Not long ago Rory had been laughing and joking with them and now this.

Ricky looked at them with frightened eyes. 'All I know is there is somebody hiding downstairs in the shadows. I came here to make a record, not end up the victim of some psychopath. Can we be sure 100% that the island was deserted? Maybe somebody has made it over here on a boat undetected before the storm or a boat took them so far and they swam in here.'

'Yeah. It's a possibility. Maybe they planned to burgle the house and got disturbed by Rory or the kids and panicked,' added Ray.

'That is possible, also, I suppose. But I have a problem with that theory,' said Ricky.

'What?' asked Ray.

'It's the manner in which they were killed.'

'What do you mean, Ricky?'

'It was like whoever killed them had planned it and enjoyed what they'd done.'

Erik and Ray exchanged nervous glances. 'I want to see Rory now,' said Erik as he headed to the stairs.

'Wait!' shouted Ricky. 'Don't go down there on your own. Wait a moment for the others to return and we all will go. There will be safety in numbers.'

Erik stopped at the top of the stairs and looked back at Ricky. There were tears in the big man's eyes.

Sydney and Marshall reappeared.

'We need to contact the police,' said Ricky.

'I tried to do it already but the storm has affected the phone lines. All I am receiving at the moment is a dead tone,' answered Sydney.

'What about the two-way radio? Can you reach Barry the boatman? He could get a message to the police,' asked Ricky.

'It is also playing up. I can try again in a little while, but even if I get through, it will be impossible at the moment for anybody to get over to the island. The sea is treacherous out there.'

'Shit. Are you telling us we are isolated here with some fucking lunatic on the loose?' asked Ray.

'I'm afraid I can't do anymore and no disrespect to Ricky, but we are not clear on what has happened. So, let's not jump to conclusions until we have all taken a look,' answered Sydney.

Ricky stood up abruptly and angrily said, 'I know what I fucking saw, Sydney. Don't treat me like a fool.'

Sydney went to pacify him but Erik suddenly spoke. 'What is that noise?'

Everybody stopped talking and listened.

'It sounds like a film rolling in the cinema,' said Sydney.

'There was one rolling earlier when I was down there. Our 1983 concert at Madison Square.' Said Ricky.

'I think we should all head down and check it out,' said Marshall.

'I agree,' said Sydney. 'But keep close together. With the lights back on it will be hard to hide if there is somebody down there.'

'If I am going back down there, I want some sort of weapon with me. If I find the fucker, I am going to batter them,' said Erik. He headed off.

'Where are you going?' asked Ray.

Erik looked back over his shoulder. 'To Harvey's room of curiosities to borrow some hardware.'

Five minutes later, with the four men armed, they all warily descended the stairs. Music still blasted out and the band recognised their track "Into the Storm" playing out. How appropriate. As they passed the cinema door, they all stole a glance inside and saw three figures sat in the front row watching the same movie that had been playing earlier.

'Who the fuck is that?' asked Ray. 'I thought you said the place was empty, Ricky?'

'I don't know who it is, it was empty when I last passed it. Although I wasn't fucking taking a stroll at the time.'

'Let's find out who these motherfuckers are,' replied Marshall, brandishing a wicked-looking samurai sword.

'Wait a second, be careful,' warned Sydney, but it was too late.

Marshall had already gone into the cinema and Erik followed, armed with a battleaxe and living up to his nickname of the Viking. Marshall was well known for his hot-headedness over the years in the band. Time hadn't seemed to have mellowed him that much. His biggest claim to fame was when an angry fan jumped up on stage at a concert in Texas and swung a punch at Marshall.

Marshall had responded by hitting him full in the face with his guitar, knocking the man off stage into the arms of security. The best thing about the whole incident was he didn't miss a note of the song the band were playing at the time. Ironically, it was a cover of the iconic record "Smash it up" by the punk band The Damned.

The two men ran straight up to the front row and confronted the figures sat there in the darkness. At first glance, they resembled dummies or mannequins, but as they got closer to them, they realised that they were real people.

'Right, who the fuck are you and what is going on?' shouted Marshall.

The figures didn't move. They sat perfectly still, their features obscured in the shadows, carrying on seemingly to watch the closing moments of the concert, taking no notice of the two men.

Marshall leant forward and grabbed the nearest person by the jacket lapels. 'I said—' His words were suddenly cut short. He then recoiled in horror as he stared into the waxy pale features of Rory. He let go of the jacket as if it was on fire and staggered backwards. Marshall now saw the other two were Kerry and Jude. Both had their throats slashed.

Erik, who was closest to Rory, seemed to have gone into shock and just froze to the spot. As the others arrived, Ricky cried out, 'Dear God, the sick bastard has dragged them out of the tub and pool and put them here. Why in God's name?' Ricky then looked around the cinema and shouted out, 'Show yourself, you wacko. Come on. Where are you?'

Erik suddenly let out a chilling howl of pain and then shouted, 'If I find the motherfucker, I will kill them.

I swear.' He was only greeted by the cheering of the crowd as the concert on screen concluded.

Sydney looked at Ricky. She touched his arm. 'Show us where you originally found them.'

Ricky regarded her momentarily with wild eyes and then nodded. 'This way.'

They gathered by the pool. A cloud of crimson resembling a large plume was spread out in the water.

'Jesus Christ,' muttered Ray.

'We need to call the fucking police,' said Ricky.

'That is not possible at the moment. I told you this,' replied Sydney. 'The phone lines are still dead.'

'But the lights are on.'

'The phone lines are on a different circuit and it keeps tripping. There must be damage somewhere outside but it is too dangerous at the present to look,' replied Sydney.

'Well, it isn't exactly fucking safe in here, is it?' commented Ray.

'This blows your theory of a random burglary gone wrong, Ray' said Ricky. 'Whoever this bastard is has planned this and he is now enjoying every fucking moment of it.'

'The two-way radio system, can you try it again?' suggested Erik.

'I can give it another go but the weather conditions are so extreme I don't even know if it will pick up a clear transmitter signal,' answered Sydney. 'Storms produce significant amounts of atmospheric noise which appears as background static in HF broadcasts. In extreme storms this can drown out voice transmissions, making communication challenging.'

'Try it, Sydney,' urged Ricky. 'See if you can get a message to Barry the boatman, please. These are our friends, for Christ's sake.'

'I am not trying to be obtuse, Ricky, but as I said earlier to the others, even if I get a call through to Barry or the police, nobody will be able to make that crossing tonight in a boat or in the air. They would also die. We are facing extreme conditions.'

Ricky stared into Sydney's face. 'So what you are saying is basically we are stuck on this island with some fucking lunatic on the loose.'

Sydney said nothing.

Marshall now intervened. 'Before you do anything, whilst we are all together, shouldn't we just check the spa and make sure nobody is hiding in there. Also, the wine cellar and studio. Maybe we can catch this fucker ourselves. If not, let's shut the bottom floor off and lock it down until the police can come; maybe we can trap whoever it is down here.'

They all agreed that this was a good idea and with some trepidation, headed to the spa room.

'Nothing,' declared Ricky. 'It is empty. Even the cover is back on the tub again. The towels are gone and so are the glasses and ashtray, and even the stupid mask Rory was wearing has disappeared. Whoever did this is one clever bastard.'

They headed to the wine cellar but it was locked as it should be.

At the studio, Sydney switched on the light. Everything seemed in place until Erik pointed to the main console. 'What the fuck is that doing there?'

Everybody followed his pointing finger to see a black Stetson sitting there. The band glanced nervously at each other. The hat was exactly the same as the trademark one Jimmy Parish used to wear.

'Right, let's go upstairs and touch nothing else. I will try the radio,' said Sydney.

They all headed back in silence. As they passed the cinema, the film had finished and the screen was blank. Nobody wanted to look too long at the three corpses in the front row.

'Does somebody have to switch the film off when it comes to an end?' asked Erik.

'No,' replied Sydney. 'Usually, the film will be on a timer and it will start and finish on its own. Nobody needed. It is all computer operated.'

'But somebody would have to switch it on, right?' pressed Erik.

'Yes,' she conceded.

'Where is the projection room?' asked Ray.

'At the back of the cinema there are some steps leading up to it,' answered Sydney.

Before she could say anymore, Erik and Marshall headed back to the cinema. When the others caught up, Erik appeared at a small window above the auditorium. 'Somebody had been up here recently. There are a couple of recently smoked cigarettes in an ashtray by the projector.' He stared down at Sydney. 'There has to be somebody in this house that is not accounted for. Is this some sick scenario your boss has instigated?'

'Of course not. Mr Barnes went to great lengths to make sure nobody, and I mean nobody, outside of this circle knew you were coming here. I am truly sorry for what has happened to your colleagues and friends. I am at a loss to give you an answer and, believe me, I want to be out of here as much as you. I suggest for now we go back upstairs and regroup. As soon as it is possible, I promise to get you all off the island,' she said.

Everybody assembled back outside the cinema. Sydney pulled the doors shut. 'For the moment, gentlemen, I am going the lock the downstairs doors to this bottom floor and try to preserve the crime screen as much as possible, until we finally get in contact with the police.'

'What about the bodies? We can't just leave them,' said Erik.

'We will have to so that we don't destroy any DNA evidence,' answered Sydney.

'Well, they aren't going anywhere,' said Marshall. Erik shot him a death stare and Marshall raised his hands as a sign of apology.

Nobody spoke, they just all grimly headed up the staircase, glad to put some distance between themselves and the bodies.

Upstairs, they gathered in the drawing room and all of them poured themselves a brandy.

'Right, I am off to Mission Control to use the radio,' said Sydney.

'I will come with you,' offered Ricky.

'I am sorry, Ricky, but that part of the house is strictly off limits to guests.'

'Fucking hell, Sydney. I would say, to quote you, these are extreme circumstances. There are three people dead and some nutjob hiding in the house. Can you not break protocol just once?' retorted Ricky.

'I am afraid not; Mr Barnes gave me strict instructions that under no circumstances does anybody enter it.'

'What if this killer is waiting for you out there somewhere, have you thought of that?'

Sydney reached into the pocket of her sou'wester and took out a small, pearl-handled .22 revolver. 'I have that covered.

Mr Barnes kindly let me have this from his private armoury of guns. He likes to practice target shooting from time to time here on the island. He gave me this Walther .22 for self-protection, especially as, sometimes, I am alone in the house arranging things for the next guests arriving. It is the perfect gun for a female and fits snuggly into a smaller hand. It really is only a precaution. I have never had to use it and, as I said, the island is pretty well protected.'

The others regarded the gun. 'No disrespect, Sydney, but do you know how to use that?' asked Erik.

Sydney smiled. 'Oh yes. Mr Barnes has given me tuition and shooting a gun seems to be in the family DNA. My father used to be an avid collector of guns.'

'Who the fuck was your dad, Buffalo Bill?' asked Marshall.

Sydney didn't answer. Instead she said, 'Right, if that is all, I am off.'

Ricky intervened. 'Just one last thing. As you said, the island is well protected and according to you uninhabited.'

'That is correct.'

'Well, if that is true, we have to face the high probability then that whoever killed Rory, Jude and Kerry is one of the gathered group in this house.' Everybody was silent for a moment.

'If that is a possibility, in that case, you were the last person to see them alive and we only have your word that somebody else killed them.' With that, Sydney then turned on her heel and walked off, calling back over her shoulder, 'I will be back as soon as possible. I suggest you all stay in the drawing room for now and lock the door behind me.'

When Sydney left, Ricky looked at the rest of the band. They stared back at him silently. 'What?'

asked Ricky. 'You think I killed Rory and the others, do you?'

The three men laughed nervously. 'No, of course not. That is crazy,' said Marshall.

'Right, in that case, I think we need to wake up the rest of the guys and put them in the picture. For all we know, they could be dead in their beds as we speak.

'Shit, Ricky,' exclaimed Ray. 'Don't say that. It freaks me out.'

Ricky regarded him and then the others. 'We have to face facts here. Somebody has maybe got us here on the pretence of making this album but what if it was all just a cover to assemble us on a remote island and murder us all.'

'Fucking hell, that sounds like something out of an Agatha Christie novel, man,' responded Ray.

'Maybe, my friend. But it isn't as far-fetched as you think.'

'OK, Ricky. Let's say that is true. Why? What is the motive? We are a veteran rock band, for fuck's sake, not a bunch of terrorists, serial killers or paedophiles. Sure, we all have done the excesses of a rock star but have you done something so bad that would warrant your life being taken?'

Ricky poured another drink but remained silent, his mind was working overtime. He swallowed his whisky in one and let the fiery liquid burn a path to his stomach. The cigarettes niggled him. It was a direct connection to Jimmy. So was the hat. Was this something to do with Dublin? No, it couldn't be, only he and Jimmy knew about Dublin and Jimmy was dead. Wasn't he? Suddenly a bizarre thought slipped into his mind. But it was too far-fetched and crazy. He immediately dismissed it. 'Right, let's head upstairs and wake the others,' he said.

'Sydney told us to wait here,' said Ray.

Ricky began to leave the room. 'Come on, man, is she your mother? We need to wake the others now. I have a feeling Ms Rose can look after herself.' He headed for the stairs that led to the upper floor with the other three soon in tow.

The three men walked along the landing and came first to Bernie's door. Ricky knocked on it three times before he heard footsteps approach it. Then they heard Bernie's voice tentatively ask, 'Yes, who is it?'

'It's me, Ricky. I am here with Ray, Marshall and Erik.'

'Do you know what time it is, Ricky? What do you want at this hour?'

'Can we please come in, Bernie? It's an emergency.'

There was a moment's silence and then the key turned in the lock and the door was opened by a sleepy-looking Bernie clad in a purple silk kimono with gold trim. 'Come in. This better be good.'

Ricky walked over the threshold with Marshall. He turned to Ray. 'Take Erik and go wake the others and bring them here.' Ray nodded. Ricky shut the door and faced Bernie.

'Well ,what is it, Ricky?' asked the older man.

'Sit down a minute, Bernie, will you.'

Ricky nodded to the minibar. 'Marshall, get us all a drink.'

Bernie sat down on the edge of his bed. 'I have a feeling whatever you are about to tell me isn't going to be good.'

'What the hell is going on? asked Jerry Fuller. The man wasn't impressed with being woken up.

'Just come with us to Bernie's room quickly, will you?' said Ray.

Jerry regarded the two men. 'Is this something to do with that clown, Rory?'

Ray looked at Erik and then back to Jerry. 'In a way it is.'

'I fucking knew it. OK, give me a moment to find my robe and I will go down there.'

'Right. We are off to wake the others,' said Erik.

Brody Willis answered quickly and told the men he couldn't sleep with the storm raging. He seemed glad for the interruption and headed to Bernie's room with the minimum of fuss.

Last up was Aadesh's room which was at the end of the corridor. They knocked the door several times without reply.

'Now what?' asked Erik.

Ray tried the door handle and it turned, opening the door. Both men regarded each other and then swallowed hard. The room beyond was in darkness except for a small artificial candle glowing in a jar by the bedside. The heavy drapes were drawn tight. They stepped over the threshold.

'Aadesh. Are you awake? We need to talk,' said Ray. They heard nothing but the unrelenting storm outside.

Ray and Erik, with some trepidation, went into the room and found the light switch. The room was suddenly flooded in brightness. The bed was empty but had been slept in. The cover was thrown back and an open paperback book lay on the duvet. As Erik passed it, he noticed it was a book entitled *Talking with Serial*

Killers by Christopher Berry Dee. They both noted the bathroom door was shut.

'I don't like this,' said Erik.

Ray looked into the frightened eyes of his friend. 'Neither do I, man, but we are going to have to open that door.'

Both men walked slowly to the bathroom door. Ray knocked on it. 'Aadesh, are you in there, mate?' There was no reply.

Ray, with his hand on the door knob, regarded Erik. The other man nodded. Ray turned the handle and pushed the door wide open and found the light switch. They scanned the room. It seemed normal. The only thing slightly disturbing was the shower curtains were drawn around the bath. Both men looked at each other again. Their eyes were wide with fear. Tentatively they walked across towards the shower.

'Aadesh, mate, are you in here?' asked Ray. Ray reached out for the curtain; his hand was shaking.

Erik stood back with the axe raised in readiness. He nodded to Ray who ripped back the curtain. The bath was empty. Both men were relieved but also concerned as to where Aadesh was.

When Ray and Erik returned to Bernie's room, both their faces were ashen.

'What has happened?' asked Ricky.

'It's Aadesh. He is not in his room,' said Ray.

'Maybe he couldn't sleep and went for a walk?' enquired Brody.

Erik scorned the remark. 'What, in this fucking weather?'

Brody immediately defended his remark. 'This house is big enough to stroll around. He might have gone to the kitchen to get a drink or snack.'

The room was silent. The storm was still raging outside and it rattled the window's in their frames.

Finally, Bernie spoke. 'We need to find Sydney and tell her Aadesh is missing and we have to get off this island now. It is not safe for any of us to be here.'

'She has gone to Mission Control, wherever that is. She wouldn't let us go with her. I have no idea where she is,' replied Ricky.

'Well let's fucking find her fast and sort this out,' exclaimed Marshall.

Jerry Fuller, who had been sitting quietly, now spoke up. 'I suggest, if we go looking for her, we need to be in a tight group. It's unlikely this person will attempt to attack us all. I think Bernie and Brody should stay put here and lock the door. Marshall, you stay with them. The rest of us can go and hopefully find Sydney and Aadesh, then we will come back here.'

'I want to go with you,' said Marshall.

'Look, Marshall, you are better off here keeping these two company and adding a bit of muscle in case it's needed,' replied Jerry.

'Jerry's right,' said Ricky. 'Keep an eye on Bernie, Marshall. We will be back soon.'

The man conceded and nodded in acknowledgement. The rest of the group left the room. Ricky looked back at Marshall. 'Don't open this door until we get back.'

'OK, Ricky. Be careful, man. Do you think Aadesh is OK?'

Ricky looked into the concerned face of Marshall. 'I don't know, mate. I honestly don't know.'

Jerry, Ricky, Erik and Ray began to walk back down the hallway towards the next staircase that led up to the band's rooms at the top part of the house. 'I think we need to explore the turret rooms. We haven't seen those yet, nor did Sydney mention them so my bet is that Mission Control is housed in one of them,' said Jerry. The other's nodded.

As the four men began to ascend the stairs, the lights flickered and went out once more. The house was plunged instantly into blackness and they all reached for their mobile phones, searching for their torch apps, none of them wanting to admit they were scared.

***

Aadesh stopped momentarily pouring milk into a mug as the kitchen lights dimmed and disappeared into blackness. The storm had indeed kept him awake and he had decided to come down to the kitchen and make some warm milk to bring back to bed in the hope that it would help him sleep. He now slowly made his way to the huge fridge where he had got the carton of milk from and opened the door in the hope that the interior light worked. It did. *It must be on another circuit,* he mused and breathed a sigh of relief.

Aadesh was grateful for the comforting light as he wasn't a big fan of the dark. As a child, he slept with a night light on until he was at least 12 years old. His father ridiculed him for this but his mother, rest her soul, kept the light burning for him no matter what. Being the youngest of four children, and the only boy, she doted on him and in retrospect, Aadesh now realised how she had mollycoddled him far too much. When he was 14 years of age, she died tragically of breast cancer. Aadesh was devastated. His father, who was a strict disciplinarian, soon toughened his son up and prepared him for the real world outside the comfort of his home in the tough suburb of Wembley in north west London. Aadesh had proven that he could be a resilient character when he needed to be. That said, even into adulthood, he still didn't sleep in complete darkness.

He now waited by the fridge door, hoping the lights would come back on soon. A nearby noise suddenly startled him. It sounded like somebody had opened and shut a drawer or cupboard. Aadesh turned around to the source of the noise but couldn't see in the enveloping blackness. 'Hello. Who's there?' he asked. He noticed his voice had a slight tremor to it. There was no reply but he thought that he could sense a presence nearby. 'I said is there anybody there?' No reply. 'Rory, is that you, man, fooling about? If it, is I am not impressed.'

No response again.

Aadesh began to feel unnerved as he thought he could detect the sound of breathing. His late-night reading material had spooked him a little. Especially now he was away from the comfort of his warm bed. He wondered if he could find his way back to his room in the darkness. He wasn't keen on having to do this. A faint squeak of a shoe confirmed to him somebody else was in the kitchen. 'Rory. This isn't funny.'

Slowly he closed the door of the fridge and darkness closed in like a cloak around him. Although he hated to do this, he surmised the darkness would envelope him and make him harder to find as he suddenly felt like somebody had poured freezing cold water into his veins. He felt like his younger self of years past. He could feel his legs shaking. He began to slowly back away, feeling blindly with his hands until he gripped the stainless steel work top of the long bench where the food was prepped. His heart beat like a hammer in his chest.

He recalled back as a child, fearing that there was a monster in his bedroom's wardrobe and how his mother would open it and assure him there was nothing there. But as soon as she turned out the main light and left the room, he was sure he saw the door edge slightly open in the shadows cast by his night light.

Aadesh felt an overwhelming urge to run but his jelly legs weren't obeying. As he whispered a silent prayer, the lights came back on. Aadesh blinked as his eyes adjusted to the sudden brightness and he saw the figure stood silently in front of him. 'What are you doing creeping around in the darkness? I thought you—'

The razor-sharp kitchen knife plunged into his throat with such force that it exited through the brain stem at the base of the skull. Aadesh was dead before he hit the floor. A look of surprise was etched upon his features. The figure stood motionless, looking down at the body of Aadesh. Blood was beginning to spread out around his head like a halo. The figure bent down, grabbed Aadesh's legs and dragged him off along the floor like a rag doll.

* * *

'Thank fuck those lights are back on,' exclaimed Ray.

The four men stood in the upper hallway.

Jerry immediately took charge again. 'I suggest we split into two groups of two. Ricky and Erik search the west side of the house and Ray and I will search the east. There are turret rooms each side so there must be another staircase to them that Sydney hasn't shown us, which could lead us to this Mission Control. Let's meet back here in half an hour.'

Everybody checked their watches. They then paired off and headed in their allocated directions.

'What the fuck do you think is going on, Ricky?' asked Erik when they were out of earshot.

'I don't know. But what I do know is we can't stay in this house. There is a killer amongst us and we are all vulnerable.'

'Who, though? We all know each other. I realise some of us don't always see eye to eye but mostly the backchat is banter. I don't see a murderer in the group. I am still more inclined to believe the theory that somebody has got onto the island undetected,' replied Erik.

'Maybe. I am not sure,' answered Ricky as they walked further down the passageway.

Erik continued. 'Barnes has a lot of seriously expensive things here well worth a seasoned thief having a go at.'

'I hear what you are saying, Erik. But most seasoned burglars do not kill people,' replied Ricky

'Maybe Rory, Jude and Kerry unfortunately discovered whoever it was and they were killed by this devious bastard. For all we know, they could have left the house and island by now as they realised somebody is living in the house.'

'Not in this fucking weather, Erik. They are trapped here just like us, and, besides, if it was just a spontaneous killing, why move the bodies and sit them in the cinema like fucking dummies? Whoever it is, is toying with us. No, whoever did this, as I said, fucking enjoyed it. These are not some hurried, random killings. It could be some nutjob who follows Barnes' blood and gore horror films and decided in their sick minds that it would be fun to re-enact some of the shit for real.'

Erik nodded and glanced around him.

Both men carried on to the end of the passageway where it turned right into another. Neither of them had been this far before. When leaving their rooms, they had naturally headed for the staircase which eventually brought them downstairs; they had no reason to explore the top floor fully until now.

Jerry and Ray had also found another passageway at the opposite end of the corridor. There were no doors visible, just walls adorned with various art work. They began to walk along it, discussing what had happened.

'So, you saw the bodies, did you?' asked Jerry.

Ray nodded. 'I have never seen a dead body before,' said Ray. 'Well, I saw my parents briefly at the funeral home, but not a person who has been murdered. Christ, I can't believe Rory is gone.'

Jerry glanced at Ray. 'It's shit, Ray, and nobody would wish that on any person but it's the two youngsters I feel for; they had their whole lives ahead of them. At least Rory had seen the best of his.'

Ray turned on Jerry. 'You unfeeling prick. So that makes it all OK, does it? I care about those kids as much as you but Rory has been my close friend and fellow band member for as many years as I can remember. We were like brothers. That is something somebody like you wouldn't understand. That's why you are on your fucking own, man.

Jerry raised his hands. 'Hey. OK, Ray. No offence intended, pal.'

'Don't fucking "pal" me; we all know you didn't like Rory. So don't pretend that his death concerns you.'

'Now wait a second, Ray, that's out of order. I came here to do a job, the same as the rest of us, and Rory fucked up. What am I supposed to do, just let it go? I am the producer and the buck stops with me. He fucked around too much since he came here for my liking but that is on a professional level. Nothing more.'

'Bollocks,' spat Ray as he swung a punch at Jerry, who easily moved out of the way of it. He then smashed his own right hand into Ray's face, putting him on his ass.

'I can see you're upset so I suggest you fuck off back to your bandmates. I can handle things here by myself,' said Jerry.

Ray looked up from the carpet, dabbing at his bloodied nose with the end of his shirt. 'Good. Piss off, Jerry. I don't want to be around you.'

'Likewise,' replied Jerry

Ray watched the man disappear down the corridor before dragging himself up to his feet. He headed back the other way in search of Ricky and Erik.

Chapter 13

Bernie tried his phone for a signal for the umpteenth time and finally threw it on the bed in frustration. 'Bloody phone.'

'Bernie, you know there is no signal in the house; Sydney told you enough times,' said Brody.

'I know, I know, but I feel so bloody helpless. I feel responsible for this situation. I thought I was being clever bringing you all here to record instead of the studios of Sunset or Muscle Shoals. Isolation and no distractions, that's what I said, and now look at us. I can't believe what has happened. I feel like a sitting duck trapped in here. In God's name, who would do such a terrible thing?'

'Bernie, don't beat yourself up. How the hell could you predict this shit? We are in the safest place for now. If we have to wait until morning and ride out this storm, we are best to do it in here,' said Marshall.

'Marshall is right. God knows what is going on here but I, for one, feel better that there is a locked door between us and this lunatic lurking in the shadows.'

'That may be true, Brody, but what about the others?'

'They will be fine if they stick together and hopefully, they will get the two-way radio working and get us all out of here,' added Marshall. 'Now who wants a drink?'

As Marshall headed to the minibar, Bernie cleared his throat. 'There is something I need to tell you about Rory.

He promised me to keep it a secret but now it doesn't matter, I suppose.'

Brody looked agitated. 'What are you waffling on about now, Bernie? Spit it out if you have something to say.'

Bernie reached for the glass of Baileys Marshall offered him. 'Rory spoke with me yesterday after the incident in the wine cellar. He confided in me that he was dying of bowel cancer and we were talking about months not years. He had been struggling with his health for a while but was keeping it a secret from the band. That was why his behaviour had become a little erratic of late.'

'The poor bastard. He should have told us; we could have helped,' said Marshall.

'He was a proud man, Marshall. He wanted to do things his way.'

'Well, it's all immaterial now, God rest his soul. It is shocking what happened to him but also Jude and Kerry; they were both 22 years old, for Christ's sake. What a waste of life,' commented Brody.

'That's what I don't get,' said Marshall. 'If there is some lunatic out there with a grudge against the band, why murder the two youngsters?'

'If it is a lunatic then they don't need a reason and everybody connected to this project is fair game,' replied Brody.

The three men nursed their drinks, thinking this over, and then there was a knock on the door. They all visibly flinched.

***

Ricky and Erik came to the end of the corridor and found a locked door to the turret room. They banged on it loudly. Ricky shouted, 'Sydney, are you in there? Aadesh has gone missing we need to make radio contact and get help fast.'

He was greeted with silence.

Erik then took a turn at banging on the door and shouting but once more there was no reply. 'This is a dead end here. We have wasted our time. I can't think of anywhere else to look. Maybe Ray and Jerry had more luck. I suggest we head back towards them.'

As they both turned away from the door in frustration, they caught sight of Jerry walking up the corridor towards them. 'Jerry, did you find anything? asked Ricky. 'We have come to a dead end here.'

Jerry seemed to be walking drunkenly. He didn't answer Ricky's question.

'Something is not right,' said Erik.

The two men moved up the corridor towards Jerry. As they got closer, they saw the blood. Jerry was doing his best to try to hold his entrails in with both his hands. They were trying to escape from a gaping wound in his abdomen. His face was ashen and his eyes stared pleadingly at the two men for help.

'Fucking hell, what has happened, Jerry? Who has done this to you?' asked Ricky.

'It, it was...' Jerry's voice was almost a whisper. It was laced with pain and despair. He tried to steady himself against the wall with one of his hands. He only succeeded in leaving a slippery, bloody handprint on it as he collapsed to the floor.

Erik crouched down and felt for the carotid pulse in his neck but there was none. 'Shit, Ricky. He is dead. Jerry is dead. This is a fucking nightmare.'

Both men glanced down the corridor with frightened eyes, expecting that, at any moment, a knife-wielding lunatic would come rushing towards them.

Ricky then looked at Erik. 'Where the fuck is Ray?'

'Christ, no. Please. Not Ray as well!' exclaimed Erik.

Ricky grabbed Erik. 'We don't know anything as yet. Let's go and see if we can find him.'

'What about him?' asked Erik.

Ricky glanced at the body of Jerry Fuller. 'He is beyond our help now.'

Erik nodded. Both men clutched their weapons tightly and glanced one last time at the body of Jerry before heading back the way they had come.

***

The three men stared at each other as the knock on the door came again. Marshall slowly moved towards it and put his ear to the wood. 'Who is it?' he asked.

'It's me – Ray. Let me in, for fuck's sake.'

Marshall unlocked the door and Ray stepped inside. 'Fucking hell, Ray. What are you doing back and where are the others?'

'We split up into twos to search. I was with Jerry but he was being an asshole, sounding off about Rory, so I left him and went back looking for Ricky and Erik. I then heard a noise downstairs and thought it might be Aadesh or even Sydney but it must have just been the wind. Seeing as I was on the same level as your room, I came back here instead,' explained Ray.

'So, there is no sign of Aadesh?' asked Brody.

'Not as far as I know. We were looking for the turret rooms to see if we could locate this Mission Control,' replied Ray.

'And did you?' asked Bernie.

'Well, when Jerry was being a dick, I left him so I don't know if he found it or not and, as I said, I didn't see Ricky or Erik again.'

'Well, we can't just stay locked in this room, we need to know if the others are safe. Do you know how to get back to them, Ray? asked Marshall.

'Yeah. I can show you but Ricky said for you guys to wait here; what if they come back and we miss them?' Ray replied.

'I will stay, just in case they come back before you,' said Brody. 'I will lock the door. I will be fine. Bernie, are you staying?'

The older man shook his head. 'No. I got the band into this mess so I am going to help them get out of it, even if it is the last thing I do.'

Brody nodded. 'OK, just go get the boys back here and we will regroup and replan.'

Marshall patted his shoulder. 'OK, Brody. Sit tight. We will be as quick as we can.'

The men left the room and Brody shut and locked the door behind them. He noticed his hands were shaking. He also noticed Marshall's glass of bourbon sat on the coffee table and walked towards it. He picked it up and sniffed the amber fluid. He was immediately transported back some years ago where he would drink this stuff for breakfast. Bourbon had been his god. It had jeopardised everything he held dear. His family, friends, job and, ultimately, his long-term relationship with his then partner. It was only when a couple of policemen had answered a call that a man had been spotted trying to climb up over the Brooklyn Bridge and they had stopped him from jumping into the icy grey waters. That night, Brody had come to terms with his alcoholism and got help. It had been so long ago.

He had been sober ever since, until now, where his nerves were frayed and he feared for his life that he had reached out to an old familiar friend. Brody swallowed the drink in one and immediately had a coughing fit and thought that he was going to be sick. The moment passed and he now made his way to the minibar. All bets were off as the sweet taste of bourbon lingered on his tongue, giving him the craving for more.

* * *

Bernie, Marshall and Ray walked along the corridor towards the stairs to the upper level.

'I just don't understand why Sydney hasn't come back with any news,' said Bernie.

'Do you think something has happened to her?' asked Marshall.

Bernie looked troubled. 'I don't know, Marshall.'

The men moved on. As they passed one of the house phones on the wall, Bernie instinctively reached for it. 'I am going to try number one and see what I get.'

Ray looked at Bernie. 'I don't expect they are operating in this weather.'

'Well, the lights are back on maybe the phones are too.'

Bernie picked it up and, to his surprise, got a dialling tone. 'It's working.'

The other two men gathered around him. He pressed one and waited, then a voice answered. It was Sydney. 'Hello.'

'Thank God, Sydney, this is Bernie; what the hell is happening? We have been waiting for you to come back.'

'Sorry, Bernie. I was just ready to make my way back to you. I have been trying to get radio contact with Barry but the signal is still scrambled. I thought I had got through at one stage but lost it so I have tried over and over but with no success. I am now heading to the generator shed as the electric keeps tripping. I am going to have to get it prepared to run but it requires diesel. I may need a hand to pour it into the machine as the drums are heavy.'

'Right, well, we can help you with that. Let me speak with the others.'

Bernie relayed the news and Marshall said he would help. Sydney told Bernie to put Marshall on the phone.

'The generator is in an outside shed. If you come down through the kitchen you will eventually walk into a passageway that leads to the food storage area. You will find a side door that leads out into the gardens there is a paved area where the refuse and recycling bins are kept. The generator shed is just across the way from there. I will wait for you by it.'

'OK, Sydney, I will be there in five minutes.' Marshall hung up the call and told the others the plan.

'You are happy to go down there alone?' asked Bernie.

'It will only take five minutes and Sydney is there. If we can get that generator working then this house won't keep being plunged into darkness and that can't be a bad thing. Besides, I have this fuck-off sword. I am ready for the bastard, believe me.'

'OK, Marshall. Ray and I will carry on looking for the others and we will all meet back in the main hallway in 30 minutes, OK? Now let's have a watch-check.'

Once done, the men split up.

It didn't take Marshall long to reach the kitchen. The place was lit brightly. He immediately saw the large puddle of blood on the floor and also more smeared tracks, as if a body had been dragged away. Fear rose in his chest.

'Sydney, Sydney! Are you all right?'

He gripped the sword tightly and scanned the kitchen nervously. Marshall cautiously walked through its length and into the corridor beyond. There he saw the side door Sydney had told him about. It was slightly ajar. 'Sydney, are you here? It's Marshall.'

He was greeted by a blast of cold air which blew in a pile of leaves as the door opened wider. Marshall looked across the courtyard and saw the shed. A glow of light was coming from within. *Sydney must be in there, thank God,* he thought. He was still troubled by the blood, though, and the absence of Aadesh.

Walking the short distance was brutally tough as the force of the wind nearly blew Marshall off of his feet. With his head down and jacket collar pulled up high, he made it to the shed. Once more, the wind made it difficult to pull the door open. He had to use both hands to wrench on the handle, so he put the sword down on the ground momentarily. He ripped the door open and practically stumbled inside.

A large torch stood on a wooden bench was providing the light. He recognised it as the one Sydney had been carrying earlier. The generator stood in the centre of the shed and there were various diesel cans of different shapes and sizes dotted around it, as well as a few tools and gardening implements. There was no sign of Sydney and the generator seemed to be working now as the engine rumbled along. *That's strange,* thought Marshall.

Suddenly, the door blew open, slamming back on its hinges. This startled Marshall. The door flying open was accompanied by another pile of leaves breezing in. 'Fuck,' he murmured under his breath. He went to pull the door shut and that's when the figure appeared in the doorway. It was more of a silhouette. 'Is that you, Sydney? You managed to get the generator working on your own, then?' asked Marshall.

The figure moved closer and Marshall saw the Stetson hat, the dark hair protruding from under it, and the black overcoat. He recognised the features but it wasn't Sydney and it certainly couldn't be who he thought it was, or could it? Marshall was hypnotised by the revelation. In that moment, the figure moved forward quickly and grabbed him by the shoulders, spinning him around and clamping a hand with a grip of steel around his nose and mouth. Marshall tried to struggle but then felt a searing pain in his right kidney as a sharp blade plunged into it. He sank to his knees in agony. The figure yanked back his head by a handful of hair, exposing his throat, and withdrew the blade from Marshall's body and then sliced it across his windpipe, cutting deeply.

Before Marshall died, he looked up inexplicitly into what looked like the features of Jimmy Parish.

Chapter 14

Bernie and Ray reached the top floor. The main lights had gone out again though only momentarily this time. They were now replaced by the emergency lighting powered by the generator. They formed a ghostly glow along the corridor.

'Which way shall we go?' asked Bernie.

'Well, Ricky and Erik headed to the west side so let's try that way first,' answered Ray.

'Maybe Jerry is with them,' mused Bernie.

Ray didn't answer.

They headed up the left corridor and that's when they saw the trail of blood on the cream carpeting.

'Shit, what the fuck's happened here?' exclaimed Ray.

Gingerly they followed it around the corner to the end of the corridor and that's when they saw the body crumpled on the floor. As they got closer, they saw the blood smeared over the wall and a large pool of it soaked into the carpet around the body itself.

'It's Jerry,' exclaimed Bernie.

'Jesus. He's been gutted like a fish,' said Ray.

Although he hadn't had a lot of love for the man, it was still horrific to see him like this.

'Where the hell are Ricky and Erik?' asked Bernie.

Ray looked further up the corridor that they were stood in. 'There is no blood beyond this point, or a sign of a struggle, so I suggest we go back the way we came.'

Bernie looked at the corpse. Jerry Fuller may have been one of those "Marmite" people you either loved or hated, but he had been a brilliant music engineer who had worked with some of the truly great artists. To see him lying stiff and grey on the floor was too much for Bernie to take. He pointed to the heavy drapes drawn on a window opposite. 'Pull those down, Ray, and cover him, will you.' Ray did as he was asked.

With one more backward glance, they walked back the way they came, picking up the blood trail once more.

'We have to get the fuck out of here, Bernie. This shit has gone really bad.'

Bernie grabbed Ray's arm. 'We will, Ray, but we need to find Ricky and Erik then we will meet up with the others and get out of this house. No matter what the weather is like, I will take my chances lasting out there until sunrise.'

'I agree.'

The blood trail led around the corner of the main corridor into another, leading to the east side of the house. It continued on. Up ahead was an oak-carved cabinet and lying on the floor next to it was a vase with flowers spilling from it. Thicker bloodstains marked the carpet. Beyond that, the trail again ended.

They now came to a turret room door and Ray turned the wrought iron circular handle. The door creaked open revealing a winding stone staircase going upwards. Small flickering artificial lights in the form of candles glowed on the walls to illuminate the way.

They heard footfall and voices above them. Both men cautiously began to ascend the stairs.

***

Brody looked out of the bedroom window. The storm still raged. He was glad that the lighting seemed to be more stable as he hated the thought of being plunged into darkness on his own. He had a pleasant buzz from the additional three miniature bottles of bourbon he had drunk, but he needed more. Aimlessly, he checked his phone for a signal but there were no bars visible on the screen. No surprise but it occupied his hands. Although slightly pissed, he was still in a state of anxiety waiting for the others to return.

He couldn't help a selfish thought entering his head. If this crazy person had a grudge against the band, then maybe he would be OK. He was just the producer. He had no major ties to Stormtrooper. To be perfectly honest, he wasn't a particular fan of theirs. He was here to do a job. Nothing more, nothing less. Then why did Jude and Kerry die? Wrong place, wrong time. They didn't know Rory was going to surprise them at the spa. The more he thought this over, the better he began to feel. Maybe he would get off this godforsaken island but hanging around with the others may now not be so smart. Brody decided to head back to his own room. He pocketed his phone and left.

Once in his room, he raided the minibar and sank three more bottles of bourbon. He then put on his coat and packed up his travel bag and left. He walked unsteadily downstairs to the hallway. It was empty. Brody thought about where he could go for safety. His hunger for more booze, though, took priority. The bourbon had given him a big dollop of Dutch courage.

He made his way downstairs, intending to go to the barroom but found the double doors leading there locked. He cursed. If he was to venture out into the storm, he didn't want to do it sober. He now decided to go to the kitchen they were bound to have some alcohol there. Brody found the kitchen also empty and quiet. Being in the centre of the house, it was shielded from the howls of the wind. He smelt a strong odour of bleach as if the place had recently been cleaned. It was so quiet he could hear the ticking of the wall clock. The time read 2.15am. If he could find somewhere to hide out where the others couldn't find him and last until daylight, then he would be safe. Fuck them, it was every man for his self now. Brody's tough New York upbringing took over. He looked in numerous cupboards, not sure which one might have what he needed. He then went to the large, industrial fridges and freezers.

The first one he opened was a freezer containing meats of all descriptions. Beef, steak, lamb, pork. No good to him. Brody needed to find a fridge. His hands were trembling; he was in desperate need of another drink. He went to the next appliance and pulled the door open. It was another freezer. The only thing it contained was the corpse of Aadesh, which stood upright in a semi-frozen state. Brody jumped back in horror as the body tipped forward towards him. He tried to move out the way but wasn't quick enough. The body of Aadesh fell out and into his arms. The sudden weight made him hit the floor with a solid thud. The corpse landed on top of him. Particles of red ice sprayed everywhere. Brody screamed and frantically flailed out until he pushed the body away.

Momentarily he lay there, panting breathlessly. He suddenly felt sick and turned his head and vomited violently. Then he rolled over and got to his knees, staring with horror at the corpse. *My God, poor gentle Aadesh. He wouldn't have hurt a fly. Clever, witty, driven and ambitious, with a thirst for life.* Brody had invested time and effort showing the younger man the business of record producing as he had joined him fresh from university. As he had got to know and work with him, he had been sure one day he would fill his shoes. He had been like a son to Brody. He felt tears well up in his eyes and he crouched over the body and began to sob. He couldn't remember the last time he had cried; he hadn't even shed a tear at either of his parents' funerals. But here and now he felt a great sorrow and loss.

Finally, he ceased his sobbing and slowly got to his feet. He found that he was trembling, all thoughts of booze gone. He now felt totally sober. Brody felt panic rise inside. Aadesh had nothing to do with the band but he was also dead. He knew he had to get out.

He turned and ran but slipped on the recently mopped floor. He crashed to the ground, landing heavily on his left shoulder. He howled with pain. Brody took three attempts before he finally found his footing on the slippery tiles. Running from the kitchen and back into the hallway, he headed for the front door. He unlocked it and pulled it open and was immediately hit by a blast of cold air and pelting rain. Brody pulled his coat around him tightly and pushed forward into the storm, the alcohol in his veins urging him on and dulling the pain in his shoulder. He didn't know where he was heading but he did know he had to put distance between himself and the house. He didn't want to die. Not here, not like this. He then thought of the outhouses Sydney had mentioned on the island; maybe he could seek refuge in one of them. But it was so fucking dark. He needed a torch otherwise he might wander off and over the cliffs.

Brody decided to go back inside and see if he could find one in the hallway cupboards or drawers. There had to be one there. Once on the porch, he pulled the door handle and found the door locked. He tried again. Nothing. How could this be? He had just gone out of it a few moments ago. Panic rose as he pulled again at the door. 'Shit, shit, shit. Please open.'

He was so engrossed in what he was doing that he never saw or heard the shadowy figure walk up behind him. He certainly couldn't stop the hatchet that came down in one fatal blow and split his skull open like an overripe melon. Brody was dead before he hit the wet ground.

The figure had some trouble pulling the weapon free from his head but finally managed it. They then stepped over the body and entered the house. The door was again unlocked. Once inside, they shut and locked it behind them. They now stood in the hallway listening. Above, they heard a faint sound of voices and silently made for the stairs.

Chapter 15

Bernie and Ray reached the top of the staircase and looked into a sparsely furnished circular tower room. They were relieved to see Ricky and Erik. They appeared to be trying unsuccessfully to break the lock on another smaller inner door. They were so preoccupied with the task at hand they were both unaware that the other two men were in the room with them until Bernie spoke. 'Thank God you are both safe.'

Ricky and Erik flinched and span around. Their eyes were wide with fear until recognition dawned.

Ricky breathed a sigh of relief. 'Jesus Christ, Bernie, Ray. Are we glad to see you. Jerry is...

Bernie put up a pacifying hand. 'We have seen him, Ricky.'

'Right. OK then.' Ricky seemed to be struggling with his thoughts.

Erik now spoke. 'We followed the trail of blood back here. We found the bottom door to this room open and came upstairs to here but it was empty. Then we saw this padlocked door and have been trying to open it, but with no luck. We were convinced that Mission Control was here, but it is fucking hopeless.' As he said this, both he and Ricky threw down their weapons in frustration.

Bernie came closer. 'Listen, guys. We have spoken to Sydney on one of the house phones. The internal ones are working again at present. There is still no radio signal and she has now, it seems, started up the generator. Marshall went to help her. I suggest we all go join them as quickly as possible.'

'Where is the generator situated?' asked Ricky

'Down beyond the kitchens,' answered Ray.

'Before we go down, I have something I need to say,' replied Ricky.

Bernie looked at the concern on his old friend's face. 'All right, Ricky, what is on your mind?'

'Since I have been in this house, I have experienced some odd things.'

Ray laughed nervously. 'That is a fucking understatement, brother.'

Ricky shook his head. 'No listen. You don't understand.' He went on to explain about the burning cigarette in his room and the packet of Marlboro Lights. The same cigarette again by the hot tub and the Stetson hat. Then the shadowy figure in black, wearing the hat.

'What are you trying to say?' asked Ray.

'Don't you see? It's Jimmy. He is here and taking some terrible revenge out on us.'

'Ricky, for fuck's sake, listen to yourself, man. Jimmy Parish is dead. We all know that.'

'Do we though, Ray? Do we? We all presumed that but what if that is not the case?'

'All right, Ricky. If, by some miracle, that is the case... why?'

'Why what?'

Ray took a deep breath trying to keep a rein on his anger. 'Why fucking kill us all? After all this time, why? Answer me that. And if he is alive, is he really capable of the brutality we have witnessed tonight? Come on,

Ricky, get a fucking grip. Jimmy was a loose cannon but he wasn't a cold-blooded killer.'

'I know what I have seen,' replied Ricky.

'What you think you have seen. Listen, man, we have been through hell here, we can start imagining all sorts of shit.'

Bernie had been listening to the heated conversation and it made him recall something Rory had told him after the episode in the wine cellar. 'This just might not be a flight of fancy.' He had the attention of the room. He continued. 'The other night I spoke with Rory after the wine cellar incident and he told me, before he passed out in there, he saw a figure in a cowboy hat standing in the aisle watching him.'

Ray looked to the heavens in disbelief. 'Christ, Bernie. Not you as well. The amount Rory had drunk that night I am surprised he didn't see Elvis mounted on Shergar with Lord fucking Lucan feeding him sugar lumps. He was pissed out of his tree, for God's sake.'

'Maybe, Ray, so in that case, isn't it more of a coincidence that both of them said they saw a figure in a cowboy hat?' The question hung heavy in the air.

'Whatever is going on, there is somebody in this house hell-bent on murdering us and if it is not an outsider and it isn't the ghost of Jimmy Parish, we have to then consider it is one of the assembled group here,' announced Erik. The room was now silent.

Finally, Bernie spoke. 'I don't buy that. Let's find the others and see if we can discover a way off of this godforsaken island.'

Everybody agreed and began to leave the room and descend the stairs. They all kept close together. Erik's last statement all resonating in their thoughts.

***

The storm was unrelenting.

The island was being battered by huge waves. Some trees had been uprooted and others had lost most of their branches. Anything that hadn't been tied down was flying around the island somewhere. At this moment in time, it was difficult to appreciate why anybody would want to be on it, let alone buy a house situated there. In the winter months, the Hebrides could be a savage place to live unless you were born to it.

Barry Skidmore, the ferry boatman, looked out the window of his cottage in Berneray. He could see the harbour down below from his dwelling, nestling in the cliff face. The boats moored down there were taking a hiding from the grey, angry waves. His vessel was luckily sheltered in the corner of the circular horseshoe bay. For now, it was safe. He had been fortunate to make the trip earlier over to Ruma and pick up the passengers and bring them back to the mainland safely before the weather turned. The storm had woken him and he was now wide awake. As he sipped on a glass of rum, he wondered how everybody was coping out on the island of Ruma.

Living in this part of the world, he was no stranger to extreme weather conditions but this particular storm was the worst he could remember in his time here. He had tried to radio through to Sydney on Ruma but with no success. The adverse weather conditions had just about interfered with everything electrical or mechanical. He hoped that they were all right out there. Barry knew what these city types were like when not in the comfort of their own surroundings. Fish out of water, they were. He laughed at his own little joke. Fish out of water, very apt. Those music guys that he had taken over to Ruma didn't exactly look like they were cut out for island life or having to tough it out if the electricity went down. They were meant to be some sort of big shots. Barry had never heard of them. *Give me Sinatra any day, or Tony Bennett.*

Mind you, Barry wasn't so keen on the island himself. Although he had ferried people out there for some years, he had never actually walked on Ruma and had no desire to do so. Growing up in the Hebrides as a kid, he would hear the local fisherman comment more than once that they could never catch anything in the waters off the island. They said that it was cursed and that a dark force lived on Ruma that kept people away and anybody who actually landed on the island would encounter bad luck. Others thought it was enchanted and was not made for mere mortals to live on.

An Diadan house had always been the topic of intrigue and mystery since the Wallace family built it and their generations lived there. At one stage in the 70s, the then owner, Joseph Wallace, decided to open the house to the public and use part of it as a B & B to help ease the extortionate maintenance bills. They advertised the island as a tranquil and romantic getaway for nature lovers and walkers or for those who just wanted to leave the stress of the big city behind them. They even brought in a yoga guru to hold daily classes for stretching and meditation. It initially went OK and business was building from an affluent clientele from Edinburgh and Glasgow and even as far as the capital, London, looking to get away from the hustle and bustle of the big city and seek a bit of spiritual guidance.

As its popularity spread, the island began to also attract celebrities to its shores. In 1978, then famous British film star, Grant Perkins, hired out the whole house for his 50th birthday. An exclusive guest list of 50 people was drawn up to attend the party. Perkins had a reputation as a hellraiser and was more than comfortable in the company of the likes of Richard Harris and Burton, Peter O'Toole, Oliver Reed and Lee Marvin; all legendary actors and equally infamous drinkers. Whatever happened at that party that night, nobody really found out, but it ended up with the bodies of a young male and female found dead in the centre of the Callanish stones the morning after the festivities. The police went to the island and interviewed all there but nobody could say what had taken place. The boy and girl had no visible injuries and the autopsy revealed nothing untoward in their bloodstream and nothing suspect internally. Some said it looked like they had been literally scared to death. The case remains open to this day and is a story that has gone down in celebrity folklore.

Perkins was disgraced and it spelt the end of his film career. He died of liver cancer in 1998 and went to his grave protesting his innocence and that he knew nothing about the deaths of the young couple and he was not in any way responsible. The locals put it down, once more, to the bad luck of the island and an evil spirit that roamed it, angry that people had made their home there.

Soon after the incident, Joseph Wallace reverted the house back from a B & B to family dwelling and not long after that, his eldest child, Toby, took over the reins. It stayed in the family until Scott Wallace decided to sell it as he was the last of the family bloodline.

When, in 2012, Harvey Barnes bought the property, people were surprised that a famous film director would want to live on such a barren and isolated spot. Barnes said his Scottish heritage had drawn him to it and his mother would have loved the fact that he was living there, albeit only six months of the year. Sensible man. Who in their right mind would want to be over there now?

This was one of a dozen or more tales Barry knew about the island and the house. It was always a source of legend and storytelling. It was definitely a place he wouldn't want to stay, especially on a night like this. The group on the island at present were effectively stranded. Until the winds abated there was no way he could sail out there and any helicopter from the emergency services had no chance. For now, they would have to stay put.

He decided to try the radio again. Once more, he got no reply. The signal was faint but working. He refilled his glass and sat back down in his armchair. In another ten minutes he would try once again. He would feel a lot better when he spoke to Sydney. There was a lot of responsibility on the young woman's shoulders, being in charge of running that house, and she was relatively new to the job. Since Sydney had taken over as Harvey Barnes' PA, Barry had sailed her out and back from the island half a dozen times or so. She always seemed a confident person and in complete control of her job and the responsibilities that came with it. Mr Barnes obviously trusted her implicitly. Yet Barry still was worried about her being out there on the island in charge of that house. Some of her predecessors hadn't fared so well on Ruma, eventually leaving because of the isolation and silence. It can get to you if you aren't cut out for the island life.

Barry took another sip of rum and picked up the paperback book lying on the floor next to his chair. He then fished in his cardigan pocket for his reading glasses. With the wind whistling eerily around his cottage, he wouldn't be sleeping anytime soon. He would finish his chapter and then try the radio again.

***

Bernie, Ray, Erik and Ricky all congregated in the main hallway.

'I am going to find out if I can phone Sydney and see where she and Marshall are. I don't fancy traipsing around his house any more than necessary,' said Bernie. He picked up a house phone and pressed number one on the handset. All that he could hear was static. He pulled the phone away from his ear. 'Nothing but static, God damn it.'

'Let's head for the kitchen then and see if we can find this generator shed,' suggested Erik. Everybody nodded in agreement.

On entering the kitchen, all the lights blazed brightly. The men immediately couldn't fail to see the body of Aadesh lying on the tiled floor.

'Good God almighty. It is Aadesh!' exclaimed Bernie. The older man was visibly grey in pallor and he gripped Ricky's arm to steady himself.

'OK, Bernie. Steady. We can't do anything for him. It's too late. We have got to think of ourselves if we are going to get out of here alive. The killer must be nearby.'

The group walked past the corpse, affording it a cursory glance, not wanting to take in the detail of the bloodied body. At the far end of the kitchen they found the passageway that led to the side door which was blowing back and forth on its hinges. The wind howled brutally into the kitchen. At the door, the men looked across the small yard to the shed.

'That has got to be where the generator is situated. Maybe Sydney and Marshall are in there still. I see a light shining from within,' said Erik.

'Right. Bernie, Ray, wait here and don't move,' Ricky instructed. 'Erik and I will take a look.'

Bernie looked at Ricky with fear in his eyes. 'Be careful.'

Ricky nodded and headed out into the storm with Erik close behind. Both men suddenly realised they had left their weapons in the turret room.

At the shed door, Ricky shouted out above the howling wind. 'Marshall, Sydney, are you in there?'

There was no response.

He grabbed hold of the door handle. Ricky caught Erik's eye and both men grimaced in determination. Ricky ripped open the door and both entered the shed. The scene before their eyes was like something out of a horror film. The place resembled a slaughterhouse with blood splashed everywhere. The body of Marshall Myers was lying lengthways along the generator on its back, facing towards the door. His face looked directly at Ricky and Erik with lifeless eyes. The gaping wound in his throat had almost severed his head from his body. The engine of the generator made the body grotesquely vibrate as if it were still alive.

Ricky turned away from the horrific sight and vomited onto the grass outside Erik stood frozen in place, his eyes transfixed on his dead friend, his brain not fully registering the situation. The big Norwegian's world was collapsing around him. These men were his family. They had welcomed him to the band and the UK from his native country of Norway. He had nobody else in the world. No family. No partner. Panic and despair overwhelmed his body and mind.

Suddenly Ray's voice pierced his subconscious. 'Have you found them?'

This snapped Ricky out of his own shock. He ran back towards the house. 'Marshall is dead. All fucking cut up,' he shouted above the roar of the wind.

Bernie felt his legs begin to give way under him and he clutched the doorframe frantically.

Suddenly an unearthly howl radiated through the storm. Ricky looked back across the yard and saw Erik looking out into the darkness shouting out "*draugr, draugr*" and then he broke into a run and disappeared into the gardens. 'Erik. Don't be stupid. We need to stay together. Come back!' Ricky shouted at the fleeing figure.

Erik didn't stop nor look back. Ricky cursed inwardly. He knew Erik to be superstitious. When going out on stage to perform, he would always go through the same ritual of blessing himself and downing a shot of aquavit, a native alcoholic drink made from potato and grain. He also wore religiously his red bandana when he performed to bring him good luck. Ricky had heard Erik use the word "*draugr*" before. It translates to English as "ghost". He shook his head in despair in the direction of his fleeing friend, who he knew he could not stop even if he tried.

He turned and ran back inside the house. 'Erik's done a runner. I couldn't stop him,' he informed the others. 'There is also no sign of Sydney, but it doesn't look good for her. So, this fucking nightmare has just got worse. There are four of us left. The storm is unrelenting and I haven't got a clue where it is safe and I haven't got a clue who the fuck is doing this but what I do know is we are rapidly running out of suspects and my theory of Jimmy Parish is not so fucking farfetched.'

Bernie looked wary as he spoke. 'One thing I know is this is the end of Stormtrooper, even if we get out of here alive.'

Ray regarded Ricky and Bernie. 'I know this is fucking mercenary of me but if we do somehow make it out, what we have recorded already here will be legendary. A legacy. Fans will die for it, if you excuse my choice of words.

Bernie cringed at the words. 'Ray, this is hardly the time or the place. I, for one, am scared shitless and also mourning the deaths of our friends and colleagues, not thinking of some monetary gain.'

Ray held up his hands. 'Sorry, Bernie. It was just a random thought. I was out of order.'

'Enough useless talk,' interrupted Ricky. 'We need a plan, a solid plan. Let's get Brody and figure out what to do.'

'Wait, you don't suppose Brody…' Ray's words trailed off.

'Is the killer? No that's impossible,' replied Bernie.

Ray smiled nervously. 'Well, how well do you really know him outside of work? I mean *really* know him?'

Everybody regarded each other silently. Then Ray spoke again. 'Sorry, guys. I am just being an asshole. It can't be Brody. Let's go find him.'

Bernie and Ricky nodded in agreement. But the thought still hung in the air. He was the only member of their group who wasn't present at this moment.

Chapter 16

Ricky knocked on the bedroom door but with no response. He tried the handle and found the door open. He regarded the other two men with a look of apprehension on his face. Pushing open the door, Ricky saw the dimly illuminated room looked empty. The three men entered and after a brief search, decided that Brody had just left the room. They all couldn't fail to notice the three empty miniature bottles disregarded on the bed.

'He should have stayed put,' said Ricky.

Ray suggested checking Brody's own bedroom. Five minutes later, they stood back in the corridor after discovering Brody's room also empty and his belongings gone.

'Where the fuck has he gone? It looks like he was running out on us,' said Ray.

Bernie went to speak and then hesitated. Ricky saw this.

'What is it, Bernie?'

The older man swallowed hard. 'You don't suppose… No, it is a crazy thought.'

'What, Bernie? Spit it out.'

Bernie looked troubled as he spoke. 'You don't suppose Brody is really responsible for all this, as Ray mentioned a moment ago? I mean, it looks like he has fallen off the wagon. Who knows what that can do to a man?'

Ricky shook his head. 'I don't see it. Brody stood to make a lot of money out of this record deal. It doesn't make sense. Ever since I have known him, he has been a gentle giant. No, this is the work of somebody else with a totally different agenda.'

'In that case, we are back to your assumption, Ricky, that Jimmy Parish is alive and well and hell-bent on vengeance, or it's his fucking ghost,' answered Ray.

Ricky remained silent.

Bernie cut in. 'I understand your reasons for suspecting this, Ricky, but I knew Jimmy a hell of a long time. He even lived at my home for a few months. Sure, he was unpredictable and hot-headed, but a murderer? No way. No Jimmy died when he fell or jumped off that yacht.'

'Then who the fuck is doing this? Sydney?' asked Ray.

'No chance. Even if she wanted to, she wouldn't have the strength to execute these murders. This is the work of a man. I am sure of it,' replied Ricky. 'That might be true but if you haven't noticed, she is a big strong girl. Definitely not a shrinking violet.'

Ricky chewed over what Ray had pointed out. Finally, he shook his head. 'No, it just doesn't add up in my book.'

'What now then? Do we look for Brody and Erik?' asked Bernie.

'We have more chance of finding a needle in a haystack, particularly if they are running around outside. I have had a thought. Let's go down to the recording studios. The glass front of the room will ensure nobody sneaks up on us. We can lock it from the inside and we can wait it out until sunrise. I think we will be safe,' said Ricky.

'That sounds like a good call. Let's do it,' replied Ray.

The three men made their way back down the staircase to the hallway. Just as they did, they heard a loud banging on the front door and then Erik's voice call out. He sounded scared. 'Open the door. Please. Is there anybody there? Hurry, for Christ's sake.'

Bernie regarded Ricky and Ray. 'It's Erik. Let him in, he sounds in trouble.'

Ricky moved to the door. As he did so, they all heard a cry from outside.

'Be careful, Ricky,' said Ray.

Ricky hesitated, momentarily frightened of what he might find. Finally, he slid the bolt back on the door and turned the handle and pulled the door open. Erik stood there. He was drenched to the skin.

'Thank God, Erik. Get in here, you big dumb Norwegian fuck.'

Erik didn't move for a moment and then he pitched forward. Ricky had a job to hold his weight as he grabbed the big man.

'All right, bro. What's wrong?' he asked as he lowered the man face first to the floor.

Then he saw the hatchet buried to the hilt between his shoulder blades. Ricky instantly looked outside for fear of somebody coming at him. What he did see was the lifeless body of Brody, sat down, propped up against one of the dog statues, just like an ancient sacrifice to the canine devils. His head was split in two in a grotesque mask of blood and gore. Bernie and Ray also saw the bodies.

Then, from the shadows of the trees, stepped a figure.

'Shut the fucking door, Ricky, quick!' shouted Ray.

Ricky seemed momentarily transfixed as the figure walked forward. It was dressed in black and wearing a Stetson. A cigarette dangled from its lips. 'Jimmy,' whispered Ricky.

Ricky could now see the large wicked-looking hunting knife in the figure's hand. He wanted to run but he was rooted to the spot, powerless to move as the figure came closer. This was it. He was going to die at the hands of his old friend.

Suddenly he felt a hand on his shoulder pulling him inside and the door being slammed shut on the advancing figure. Ricky fell to the floor and looked up to see Ray slip the bolt across into place. He now looked to his left to see the corpse of Erik bleeding out on the carpet. Erik "the Viking" Olsen. A big strong man and a major presence wherever he went, now lying there, a lifeless shell. Ricky hung his head in his hands and tears began to run down his face. The comforting arm of Bernie wrapped around his shoulder. He then heard Ray's voice urgently tell him to get up and that they had to get downstairs to the recording studio.

Ricky got to his feet. He was noticeably shaking. 'Did you fucking see him? He was standing there. Jimmy was standing there. I told you.'

Ray gripped his arm. 'I saw somebody but I couldn't tell you who it was. Now get a grip. If we are going to survive, we need to move now.'

The trio made their way down the stairs. They came to the doors that Sydney had locked earlier. Ray grabbed hold of a fire extinguisher off the wall and smashed it down onto the door handles until it broke the lock and they pushed the doors inward. The low lights that the generator had working cast shadows everywhere and the men expected the figure to spring from the gloom at any moment. Slowly they walked past the cinema; it was now in darkness and none of them wanted to think of the corpses still sat in the front row. They now passed the bar and games room. It, too, was in darkness.

'Wait,' said Ray. 'I am going to get a few bottles to steady the nerves. If we are going to be locked in the studio for a few hours, I need a fucking drink to deal with this shit.'

'Leave it,' hissed Bernie, frightened to raise his voice.

'I will be two minutes. Trust me. I will be fine. Remember, whoever that lunatic was outside, we locked him out there, so he can't be down here, can he?'

'Hurry then,' replied Bernie.

Ricky stood silently, still in shock.

Ray opened the door and looked for the light switch. He found it and illuminated the room in a ghostly glow. He looked at Bernie's worried features. 'I will be fine. I will bring you back a bottle of Baileys.' With that, he disappeared inside and the door swung shut behind him.

Ray moved past the pool tables, making a beeline for the bar. He vaulted over it and started helping himself to a bottle of French cognac.

He, too, was in shock but did not register it. He began talking to himself. 'Yes, that will do me, thanks very much.' He unscrewed the top off the bottle and with shaking hands, took a huge gulp of the brandy. 'Woah. That hit the spot. Right, what else have we got? I can't leave my old pals out of it. Baileys next, for Bernie boy.'

As he scanned the bottles, he realised he was crying. The tears began to run uncontrollably down his face. A voice from behind suddenly startled him.

'I'll have a Jack on the rocks, "Hammer".'

Ray whirled around. He stared into a face he knew. 'What the fuck… What are you doing here—'

His words were cut short by a bottle of vodka that sat on the bar being smashed over his head. Ray staggered back, falling into the optics, blood pouring down his face from a gaping head wound. He slid to the floor, stunned. The figure walked slowly around the bar; their features blurred in and out of Ray's vision as they got closer.

'Please don't kill me. For Christ's sake. This is madness. What have I ever done to you?'

The figure picked up a corkscrew from the bar top. 'Sorry, Ray. I haven't got time to explain. Too much still to do.'

Ray wiped the blood from his face. 'You mad fucker. I—'

His words were cut off as the corkscrew was driven with considerable force straight through his left eye. It penetrated into his brain and he died instantly.

Bernie was getting concerned about Ray as he had been longer than he had promised. He was steeling himself to go look for him when music burst through the silence. Bernie instantly recognised the song as "Killer on the Loose" by Irish rockers, Thin Lizzy. The frenzied guitar riff and the velvety vocals of Phil Lynott echoed through the downstairs. The song was coming from the jukebox. *What the fuck was Ray playing at?* He looked at Ricky who was ashen-faced and staring blankly into space. 'Stay here and don't move.'

Bernie entered the room and immediately saw the jukebox lit up and glowing as the music blared out of it and then he saw Ray lying on the bar. A corkscrew was protruding from his eye. He didn't need to get any closer to know he was dead. Suddenly, fear gripped him and he turned to run but then saw the figure standing there. They were stood in the shadows and their features not recognisable but the Stetson was. 'It can't be you,' whispered Bernie.

The figure came towards Bernie, reaching for the hunting knife in the scabbard hanging from their belt. Bernie suddenly felt a burst of anger inside that triggered his adrenaline into positive action. He pushed a table into the figure's path and ran for the door. As he burst out the room, he shut the door behind him, slipping the bolt across just in time. He grabbed Ricky by the arm and shouted, 'Come on. We have to get out of here. Ray is dead and whoever did it is coming for us. You were right, it is Jimmy.' This seemed to shock Ricky from the trance like state he had been in. 'We can't head for the studio, Ricky, it will be a dead end and we will be found. We have to go back up. Come on.'

As both men headed for the stairs, they heard the weight of a body smashing against the barroom door. Bernie prayed it would hold for now. They made it back up to the main hallway. Only then did they draw breath. They looked back towards the stairs, expecting the figure to appear at any second but all was quiet.

Both men's faces looked haggard and their eyes hollow in the dim light. Neither knew what to say to each other. They were physically and mentally exhausted. The full ramifications of what had happened that night began to sink in. They were the last two from their party left. Twelve had all come here to make a record and nearly all were dead. Why, was a mystery. Had they been lured here by Jimmy Parish? Was he really alive or had this strange island inhabited his ghost from beyond the grave? Both ideas seemed preposterous but at this moment in time, both men were having a job deciphering what was reality and what wasn't.

Lucky old Kenny. He managed to escape the island. Ironically, we could have used his muscle, thought Bernie.

The grandfather clock ticking away in the corner told them the time was 4am. Another hour or so would bring sunrise. Both hoped that the storm would have died down and they could leave the house safely and get help. But first they had to survive the hour and stay clear of this lunatic.

Chapter 17

Bernie and Ricky stood in the hallway, unsure of where to head for the best. The door downstairs would not hold forever. Their eyes were heavy with fatigue. Both were mentally and physically battered. But they knew that they had to keep going. Going outside into the storm seemed the only option left but they were so tired and running low on energy. They were jolted from their lethargy by the door downstairs crashing open.

Footsteps sounded on the stairs. Both men braced themselves for the worst and then the frightened features of Sydney appeared from the library doorway. 'Quick, in here,' she shouted.

Both men were shocked to see she was still alive. They ran to the library and slipped inside. Sydney locked the door behind them. Ricky and Bernie saw blood on her hands and it was also evident on the white t-shirt she wore under her jacket. When she saw the two men, she breathed a sigh of relief. 'Thank God I found you and that you are both alive. Everyone else has disappeared. I have been hiding in here since I found Marshall dead in the generator shed. It was terrible. I ran back here and into the library. I then heard noises coming from downstairs and opened the door to find you both standing there. I thought everybody was dead.' She paused and tears formed in her eyes. 'I am so sorry for all that has happened; I swear to God I don't know who is doing this and why.'

Ricky regarded her distraught features. 'Christ, Sydney, we thought you were dead. When we came across Marshall, we presumed that you had also been killed.'

'I went to meet Marshall in the generator shed and he wasn't there so I went back into the house to wait. Ten minutes later I returned to the shed and found his body. Dear God. I just panicked and ran.'

'Are you hurt?' Ricky asked, gesturing to the blood on her hands and clothes.

'No. It was Marshall's. I tried to help him but it was too late.'

Sydney walked over to a leather wingback chair and flopped down. She also looked tired.

Bernie spoke. 'Is there still no radio signal for the boat to get us off this godforsaken place?'

Sydney shook her head. 'The storm has wrecked everything. The island is completely isolated. When dawn comes, our only hope is, if the storm has died down, that Barry the boatman will come out here to check on us.'

Both men looked at the clock. It now read 4.10am.

'Christ I could murder a coffee,' said Sydney.

'Not the best choice of words, my dear,' replied Bernie. 'But I could certainly use one as well. I am flagging, I'm afraid.'

'I am not going down in that fucking kitchen again,' exclaimed Ricky. His mind flashed up the horrific images of Aadesh and Marshall.

'I have a coffee machine in Mission Control,' said Sydney.

'Where the fuck is this Mission Control Sydney?'

She held up pacifying hands. 'I am sorry, Ricky, due to strict protocol, I couldn't tell you earlier on, but now it doesn't matter anymore. It's been just here all along under your noses. Harvey Barnes' locked study that I showed you when you first arrived. It is housed there. I was safe in there but came out to get the generator going after the house phones momentarily came back on and I spoke with Bernie.'

'Personally, I would have stayed in the study if I was safe there,' said Ricky

'I have a job to do, Ricky, and a responsibility to Mr Barnes, the house and his guests. That is why I have come looking for you.'

'Sorry,' replied Ricky.

Suddenly they heard a noise in the hallway.

'The crazy bastard is in the hallway looking for us,' whispered Bernie.

'Which means they will be heading here soon,' added Ricky.

Sydney pulled back her coat and produced the gun from her waistband. 'Then we will be ready.'

'Thank God, Sydney. You still have your gun. We have a chance if this madman finds us,' said Bernie.

Sydney stood up and went to the study door and unlocked it. 'Come on. Get in here, you will be safe.'

They all moved into the study. Once inside Ricky and Bernie appraised their surroundings. Far from being a brass and oak polished affair, it was more like the inside of a space station. The study had just been a front for the beating heart of the whole house. Hi-tech equipment and computer screens were everywhere, monitoring every part of the house, inside and out.

This was some serious surveillance equipment, thought Ricky. If Sydney had been in here all along and this kit was working, how come she told them earlier there was no CCTV around the house and also, wouldn't she be able to see them all and know where the killer was in the house? It didn't make sense, unless...

Sydney locked the door and then turned around and pointed the gun at both men. 'Both of you move on to the sofa.'

Bernie looked shocked. 'What is going on? I don't understand.'

Sydney brandished the gun menacingly in their direction. 'Be quiet and do as I say.'

Bernie and Ricky backed up to the sofa and sat down, confusion etched on both their faces.

A small smile played on Sydney's lips. 'Well, here we are, the last of the mighty Stormtrooper and, indeed, the two most important members left. That is why you have been spared until now.'

Ricky went to get up. 'What the fuck is this all about—'

A bullet smashed into the arm of the sofa and both Ricky and Bernie cowered away. The noise vibrated around the room like an exploding bomb.

'Don't fucking move. I mean it.'

Ricky raised his hands in surrender. 'Shit. OK, Sydney. What is happening here?'

Sydney perched herself on the edge of the desk. 'We have plenty of time together now, with nowhere to go, so let me tell you a story. A story that will explain why all this has happened and why you are both last. Sydney Rose is not my birth name. My name is Eve.

The name "Sydney" was given to me by the wonderful family who adopted me when I was just a very young baby. Graham and Alice Rose were the most wonderful parents a child could have wanted. They welcomed me into their family and loved and cared for me. They were so generous and kind and I had an amazing childhood growing up. They already had an adopted son two years older than me named Noah. We became very close, almost inseparable. We shared many wonderful times growing up together.

'Graham Rose, my father, piloted jumbo jets all around the globe. The family experienced many exotic holidays and saw a great deal of the world out there. Travel was in my blood and I grew up to become a cabin crew member for BA. I loved it and continued my world travels. Noah, at 18 years of age, joined the armed forces. I didn't see him so much after this but we still remained close.

'Graham died, ironically, in a car crash one foggy night driving home on the M1. He had piloted hundreds of long-haul flights with little or no incident, then this tragedy occurred. He drove into the back of a lorry that had pulled over onto the hard shoulder but hadn't put their hazard lights on. We were all devastated. A few years later, Alice developed breast cancer that spread rapidly to other areas of her body. The diagnosis was terminal.' Tears formed in Sydney's eyes as she recalled this.

Bernie and Ricky sat quietly, wondering where this was all heading.

Sydney now composed herself. 'Anyway, this is where the story gets interesting for you two. Weeks before Alice died, she asked me to come to her bedside.

This was when she told me that I had been adopted and she now felt it was the right time to let me know. I was at first shocked. I had no idea whatsoever. She told me that both my birth parents died a long time ago and that was why I had been adopted as a baby.

'My birth mother's name was Mary Gilmour. A very competent artist but unfortunately a drug addict. Her addiction claimed her life. My father was none other than Jimmy Parish, rock god and original singer of Stormtrooper. He died before my birth and never knew he had a daughter.'

Bernie and Ricky looked at each other, stunned. They hadn't known that Mary Gilmour had given birth to a child.

'Surprise, Surprise, as good old Cilla used to say.' Sydney let out a crazy laugh. 'Anyway, Alice told me that in the basement was a trunk of my father Jimmy's belongings that were offered by the authorities after both my parents died. Also, I had a bank account set up in my name for money to be deposited into from the sale of Bracknell House and other assets of my father's. I became quite affluent overnight. I briefly looked into the trunk of memorabilia but never delved too deeply. I guess I was in a state of shock at the time but I put the trunk into storage for safekeeping and, to be honest, I forgot about it. Next, I handed in my notice and embarked on my own travels around the world. I remained anonymous. The daughter of Jimmy Parish. Nobody ever knew until now.'

Bernie spoke up. 'Why now, then? Why reveal yourself?'

'Because a little while ago I read that the band was reforming and it made me remember the trunk. I got it out of storage and this time had a thorough look. I found Dad's trademark Stetson which has come in handy here as a little prop. There were a lot of other personal items which, in this day and age, would make a mint on eBay. Photos, concert programmes, souvenirs, etc., but they are not for sale. The interesting thing was I also found a couple of journals. I found out through internet research that Jimmy planned to write a warts and all book about his time in the band after he was kicked out. He planned to expose all of you with some pretty juicy stories but, unfortunately, he died before the book could be written. How convenient. His notes were forgotten and ended up in the trunk which I inherited. I read the journals completely and it told me all I needed to know about how all of you destroyed my father. You and Bernie were the main two that made it happen.'

Ricky cut in. 'Now wait a minute that wasn't how it was. We—'

'Shut up!' shrieked Sydney. She began to get agitated. 'I read everything, Ricky. I know about Dublin and what happened. How you killed that girl in some kinky sex game and how Jimmy begged you to call the police but you refused and threatened that you would kill him also, if he went against you. You then covered your tracks and the death was never connected to you. Jimmy kept his side of the bargain and kept your secret and you repaid him by not only kicking him out the band but also taking his place as lead singer. You conniving bastard.'

Both men could see the fury in her eyes.

Ricky protested, 'That is not true. I was out of it in that room. I had no idea what happened but it was Jimmy who told me that I had killed the girl. He was the one who suggested covering up the murder otherwise our burgeoning careers would have been over and Stormtrooper wouldn't have existed. He even told me he would get rid of the bandana used in her death but later revealed he still had it. He was going to blackmail me with it. When the band voted him out, that was when he decided to get his revenge and write these lies.'

Sydney interrupted, 'And that's when you decided to sneak onto his yacht the night of his birthday party and murder him.'

Ricky stood up, all fear, for the moment, replaced by outrage. 'You are wrong. I didn't kill him. I was nowhere near that boat.'

'Liar!' shouted Sydney and fired the gun.

The bullet hit Ricky in the thigh and he collapsed to the ground, clutching his leg in agony. Through gritted teeth he hissed, 'You mad bitch. You have it all wrong. If you are going to kill me, fucking kill me, but I am innocent of the death of Jimmy. God knows what happened in that bedsit in Dublin but there is not a day that goes by where I do not regret it. The poor girl didn't deserve what happened to her and I will go to my grave in remorse, but I had nothing to do with Jimmy's death. I swear.'

Sydney walked forward. 'Even now, lying on the floor like a wounded dog, you can't own up, can you, Ricky?' She levelled the gun again, ready to fire.

Bernie intervened. 'Wait, let me ask you something.' Sydney hesitated and looked his way. Bernie swallowed hard and continued. 'If you think Ricky and myself are responsible for the downfall of Jimmy, then why kill the rest?'

Suddenly, the study door opened and in walked a man. For all intents and purposes, it looked like Jimmy

Parish. The black Stetson, the long leather coat, the cowboy boots. 'Sydney didn't kill them I did.'

Sydney smiled. 'Let me introduce my partner in crime.'

As the man walked out of the shadows, he removed the hat and then the wig under it and threw them onto the console.

Bernie could now see who it was. 'Jesus Christ, Kenny. I thought you left the island.' Bernie's mind was in a whirl. 'Why? I don't understand. Kenny, why?'

'I am not Kenny Holton. I am Noah Rose. Sydney's stepbrother.' Bernie was gobsmacked. 'I love her unconditionally and I would do anything for her. We immediately bonded as children and looked out for each other always. Even when I joined the army, we stayed connected. I was always there for her and vowed nobody would ever hurt her. After I left the forces, I met up with Sydney again and we shared a flat together and our bond got stronger once more. She told me everything about her real father and what you lot did to him. She was deeply upset about what happened and she was determined to make amends. She told me her plans and she asked for my specialised skills, shall we say.'

Sydney smiled and reached out and stroked Noah's shoulder lovingly. For a moment she seemed to have forgotten about Ricky.

'I couldn't have her upset. I don't like to see her upset. People have tried to hurt her in the past but I sorted them out. Haven't I, Syd?' Noah looked towards Sydney for her approval like a puppy would to their owner.

By now, Bernie and Ricky knew they were dealing with two people who were not sane and some deep-seated childhood bond had become warped and distorted somewhere.

Sydney continued, 'We hatched a plan after we read about the possibility of Stormtrooper coming out to Ruma to record a new album. In the world of the wide web, nothing is really a secret, Bernie, as you thought. It seemed the ideal opportunity to exact our revenge here in isolation. Through my jet-setting, I knew Harvey Barnes. I was confident I could get a job from him but I needed to be close to him. I needed to be his PA. The trouble was, he had one already. Eileen Rodgers. So I made the trip to Barbados and befriended her.

'It was easy. She was a lonely, single girl, homesick for her family. Eileen was weak and vulnerable and in need of a friend. I became that friend. One night, I got her drunk at a seafront bar. After closing, we walked along the beach. It was pretty deserted. I persuaded her to go skinny-dipping. She was too intoxicated to refuse. Once out in the water, I grabbed her and held her under. She wasn't strong enough to fight me. I drowned her. I went back into shore unnoticed and the next day I flew home and waited for my chance to apply for the sudden job vacancy.

'I settled into the job comfortably and as the months went on, I gained Harvey's full confidence. I helped make all the arrangements for Stormtroopers visit. The week leading up to you coming out here, I saw the weather forecast and the gods must have been smiling on me as I knew the storm coming would isolate the island completely and make my job easier. It was perfect.'

Noah now took over. 'I pretty much did the same, applying for the vacant slot to be your personal assistant/minder, Bernie. I guess I got the position over any others because I agreed to sleep with you.'

Bernie's face reddened.

Ricky looked up at him from the floor. 'What the fuck is he talking about, Bernie?'

Bernie said nothing but hung his head.

Noah continued, 'Killing was easy to me; I had been trained in the forces to do this and I had done many times. I have seen and done shit no man should have but, in the end, you get desensitised to it. You become detached. I would do anything for my Sydney to make her happy.' Kenny glanced lovingly in Sydney's direction then his featured hardened again. 'This house has a network of secret passages that originally Harvey Barnes used as escape routes in case he was in danger. I utilised them to move in and out the house undetected and so did Sydney. We both also have sets of keys to every door. Each room, including your bedrooms, had a hidden monitor in them. We could see everything and keep track of you all at any time. It made my job easy. We agreed to add the disguise of Jimmy Parish to fuck with your minds and make you believe the ghost of Jimmy had come back for vengeance. It all worked perfectly.'

'Why kill the others? They were not guilty of any crimes,' asked Bernie.

'They were in the wrong place at the wrong time. Coming to the island to help make your record already sealed their fates. Nobody was ever going to leave alive. We would then disappear after the job was done. When the authorities finally got onto the island and saw the carnage, they would probably presume that everybody in the party were victims as we would have dumped all the corpses in the sea. We have a motorised dingy stored away on the other side of the island, close to the nesting puffins. We will make our escape from the island after we have finished with you two.'

Sydney now cut in. 'Anyway, enough storytelling.' She turned her attention back to Ricky. 'Time to die for killing Jimmy and depriving me of knowing my real father.'

Bernie suddenly stood up. 'Wait. Wait. You have the wrong man. I killed Jimmy.

Chapter 18

Sydney stopped in her tracks and now pointed the gun in Bernie's direction. 'Explain,' she said.

Bernie sighed wearily. 'First of all, I want to tell you something, Ricky. Something I knew for a long while but when Jimmy died, I just couldn't find a way to tell you. I am so sorry.' Tears formed in the older man's eyes. 'You didn't kill the girl – Shauna Daly. Jimmy did.'

Ricky sat back against the sofa and took the scarf he was wearing from around his neck and wrapped it tightly around his wound. 'What the hell do you mean, Bernie?'

'Some years ago, when we were just back from the Japan tour, Jimmy lodged with me for a while as he and Mary had a bit of how a bust-up. Regardless of things ended up between us, at one time, Jimmy was like a son to me. We were very close, but never sexually. We trusted each other. One drunken and coke-fuelled night, both of us talked and talked into the small hours. The more out of it we got, the more secrets we told each other.

'Jimmy told me about the whole Dublin affair and how he had accidentally choked the girl with her own panties in a sex game that got out of hand. Whilst this was happening, you, Ricky, were crashed out in the living room, oblivious to what was going on. At first,

Jimmy panicked and didn't know what to do. Then he began to hatch a plan to save his own selfish ass. He carried your practically unconscious body into the bedroom and stripped you of your clothes and put you into bed beside Shauna. He then removed the bunched-up panties from Shauna's mouth and replaced them instead with your neck scarf. He then left the flat and disposed of the panties and bought some cigarettes. He then came back and woke you and pinned the murder on you. You were so out of it, you didn't have any recollection, only Jimmy's word to go on, and you swallowed it.'

Ricky was stunned. 'Fucking hell, Bernie, you kept this from me? Why?'

Tears ran down Bernie's face. 'One reason was because I was a selfish bastard. If I had told you, that would have been the end of the band and Stormtrooper were just ready to hit mega stardom and untold riches. I couldn't risk you both fighting and leaving. There was too much money at stake. So I kept it a secret as Jimmy had asked me to. When he died, I just couldn't find the right moment to tell you or know whether I should. With Jimmy now dead, your problem was gone with him. Then the band later split and we all went our separate ways. I thought it better to say nothing.'

'Fuck, Bernie. I have been carrying this shit around with me for years. The guilt eating away at me and all this time it was Jimmy. You should have told me.'

Sydney cut in. 'You are lying, Bernie.'

Bernie looked at the blazing hate in the young women's eyes. 'Why would I lie?'

Noah now spoke up. 'A desperate bid to save his skin and yours, Ricky.'

Bernie laughed out loud and stood up. His fear for the moment gone. 'Kenny. You fool. I wondered what I ever saw in you.'

Sydney interrupted again. 'You said you killed my father. Go on.'

Bernie sat back down on the sofa. 'That night Jimmy confessed his crime to me, he then asked me what dark secrets I held. As I said, we were both totally wasted. Another line of cocaine went up my nose and I confessed to him that I was gay and had been since I was a young man. I grew up in a time where there was no tolerance or understanding of homosexual relationships. I tried to deny my feelings. I had got married but struggled constantly with confusion about my sexuality. I loved Kim, truly I did. I played the role of husband and father perfectly, but there was no denying that I was attracted to men.

'In the job I had as a rock band's manager, jetting around the world and being away from home for months on end, I had plenty of opportunity to indulge my passion without Kim or the kids ever knowing. Essentially, I lived two lives and I got very good at doing that. Christ, I even got the run of the house here on Ruma because Harvey Barnes and I were lovers for a short spell. I had a long-term partner named Brian. He lived in the States. We had an open relationship but whenever I visited San Francisco, we would meet up. Unfortunately, he died a little while back from cancer. I knew him for more than twenty years. I was devastated.

'I told Jimmy about my secret life. Also, at that time, I was in a brief affair with a big-name music star. I told Jimmy who it was. Jimmy knew him well. This person also was not known to be gay. I told Jimmy that he must never divulge my secrets to anybody, especially Kim and my family. It would devastate them. I couldn't have that. So, we made a pact. We wouldn't reveal either of our secrets ever. Both would destroy us if made public. It was an uneasy alliance built totally on each other's trust. This was why I was so reluctant to fire Jimmy from the band. Yes, it was purely for selfish reasons. I am not proud of myself but it was self-survival.

'There were many occasions when you, Ricky, and the others were right about Jimmy but I couldn't sack him from fear he would break the pact. Then eventually, when we did get rid of him and the book deal was offered, he rang me up and told me in the book he would reveal my secret and also the identity of my pop star lover. I couldn't have that. I pleaded with him but to no avail. I then threatened him with his confession about what had happened in Dublin but he told me there was no evidence against him and he could easily incriminate Ricky and destroy him. Plus, it would be the end of the band. I realised he had tricked me and had me over a barrel.'

Bernie looked at Sydney. 'Your father was not a nice man.' He then glanced at Ricky. 'He was hell-bent on destroying us both. So I found out the exact location of his birthday celebrations and hatched my own plan. The night of the party, I took a motorised dingy a friend of mine owned out on the water. Remember, my father had been a sailor on the Isle of Wight and I grew up with boats. I had no problem sailing or navigating the waters. I sailed out undetected to Jimmy's yacht and climbed on board just as the party moved below and waited for things to die down. Eventually, luck had it that Jimmy came up on deck. I saw he was worse for wear and knew he would be easy prey. I cut the power to the lights and crept up on him and hit him over the head with a hammer. He fell overboard into the sea. I climbed back down into the dingy and dragged his body on board. I then went back on board the yacht and raised the anchor so the boat would float away from its present location, making it difficult to pinpoint where Jimmy might have fallen in the water if the authorities suspected foul play and made a search. I then took the dingy further out to sea. I wrapped Jimmy's body in a weighted fishing net and pushed him over the side. I knew his body wouldn't rise up to the surface anytime soon. Then I went back to shore, hosed down the dingy so it was spotless and returned it to the boathouse where I got it from and locked it safely away.

'The danger of Jimmy revealing any secrets were now gone. Stormtrooper were free to go on to the global success they had and my personal secret was safe forever. My family would never have to endure the shock and disappointment of my other life or the media circus that would have followed.'

The room was silent.

Sydney then called Bernie's name and he looked up. A look of resignation was on his face. The bullet Sydney fired hit him squarely between the eyes and he slumped back onto the sofa. Blood and gore sprayed the wall behind him. The other four bullets put into him weren't needed; he was dead from the first shot.

This spurred Ricky into action. From his position on the floor, he kicked out at the back of Sydney's knee and she fell forward into Noah in a tangle of arms and legs. Gritting his teeth, he dragged himself to his feet. The adrenaline rushing through his body helped mask some of the pain from the gunshot wound. He limped as fast as possible to the study door and grabbed the handle pulling it open. He managed to get out but as he went to shut the door, Noah reached his hand through to stop it. Ricky opened the door a fraction and then slammed it onto Noah's fingers. The hand quickly withdrew and Ricky shut the door and turned the key.

He moved through the library and out into the hallway. He had to steady himself by grabbing hold of a sideboard as a wave of nausea washed over him. Ricky took a few deep breathes and the feeling passed and he made for the front door and flung it open, careful to avoid the body of Erik. He ran out into the wild night, having no idea where he was heading.

The revelations of the last half an hour resonating around his head. Bernie, Sydney, Noah, Dublin. Crazy stories. Sydney and Noah, in some lunatic family pact, coming together to wreak revenge for Jimmy's death. Sydney, seemingly obsessed with the fact her real father was the legendary Jimmy Parish, who she had been deprived of ever knowing because of his untimely death. All this blood and murder for a man whose own soul was black and was probably living it up in the fires of hell right now. The spectre of Jimmy Parish after all these years had come back to haunt them. Redemption had come to them all.

Ricky now knew he didn't murder Shauna, but he was still guilty of covering up a death. Bernie. Christ, he had hidden his homosexuality well but it did explain his outburst a few nights ago when Rory had a dig about him being gay. Had Rory suspected or had it just been a coincidence? Ricky knew how much Bernie loved Kim, his children and grandchildren. Bernie had grown up and had lived in an era that had no acceptance of homosexuality. He chose to hide it, knowing he could not break Kim's heart by confessing to her. What would be the point? Bernie had lived a life of turmoil but managed for years to keep his secret. Jimmy threatened to reveal it and this was the straw that broke the camel's back. Gentle Bernie, a killer. Who would have thought? And now, after everything, he was dead.

Ricky hobbled out of the grounds and onto the barren landscape of Ruma. He looked back to the house and saw the front door open and two torch beams split the darkness. *Shit.* They were coming for him. Luckily for him, the gunshot injury just seemed to be a flesh wound, no vital arteries or veins had been hit, so, although it hurt like a bitch, the bleeding was subsiding. Ricky looked at the illuminous dials on his watch. Half an hour would bring sunrise. He had to find somewhere to hide until it became light and then maybe, just maybe, he could find a way to escape. He wasn't willing to think of the alternative scenario.

Chapter 19

Ricky blindly edged forward. He could do with a torch to light his way but he knew that it would also give away his location. He moved slowly, the pain in his leg now a constant throbbing. Somewhere to his left he could heard the sea. Waves were crashing into the landing jetty. He tried to visualise the island's layout from memory from when Sydney had gave them a brief tour but it was difficult. He didn't know if, in this weather, he could find his way back down to the jetty to where the ferry had docked but even if he could, there was nowhere to go and he would be a sitting duck for those crazy pair of bastards. He decided to go right and make some distance from the house.

Just then, he heard a voice rise above the howling of the wind. It was Sydney. 'You can't get far, Ricky. There is nowhere to go. Even if you make it to daybreak, there is nobody here. Just you and us. There is no help coming your way. You are going to die along with the others. Nobody can be allowed to live.'

Ricky felt anger rise within him. 'Fuck you both. Somehow, I am going to get off this island and get to the police and tell them it all. You pair of crazy motherfuckers are going to be locked up and the key thrown away.'

Ricky now heard Noah's voice. 'Brave talk for a wounded man wandering around in the darkness on an island he doesn't know. Remember, I am an ex-paratrooper. In places like Kosovo and Afghanistan, my job was to flush out the enemy and kill them, period. These individuals were trained fighters; what chance do you think a washed-up rock star stands?'

Ricky knew this to be true but he had to now show bravado. 'We'll see, you fucking fruitcake.'

Ricky turned and buried his chin deep into his jacket collar and forged on. Slowly he made progress. Every now and again he would stumble on the uneven ground. But he gritted his teeth against the pain in his leg and carried on. Fear was his ally and spurred him onwards. He suddenly found himself by the Callanish stones. They stood gnarly and proud against the night sky. They were roughly ten feet in height and formed a rough circle. On the ground were also hundreds of little stones and rocks, making the ground difficult to walk on.

He moved amongst the stones. They gave him a degree of shelter from the unrelenting rain and wind. Ricky found he was shivering uncontrollably. He was soaked through to the skin. He sank to a sitting position and rested for a moment. Fatigue made him bone weary. The blood loss didn't help matters and it worried him that he would get too weak to carry on and just lie down and let Sydney and Noah extract their revenge without any sort of fight. Ricky thought of all his bandmates. Every last one of them dead. Murdered horribly. Poor old Bernie, also gone. Bernie, who had been responsible for the death of Jimmy. Bernie, who lived a double life and could not allow himself to be exposed. He had carried that secret and the secret of Dublin around with him for many years. They probably would have gone to the grave with him until Jimmy's daughter came on the scene and her crazy stepbrother. Kenny Holton was a crafty little shit. He wormed his way into the inner sanctum of the band and also into Bernie's affections. All that time he was plotting Stormtrooper's demise, all because of some weird, unhealthy obsession with his stepsister and her warped crusade to avenge a dad she didn't really know but had benefited greatly from in a financial sense due to his and Mary's death. He could hardly believe all this had happened. It was just like a Harvey Barnes film.

Ricky found his eyes beginning to close. Suddenly, a voice near to him jolted him awake. He had allowed himself to succumb to sleep and had stupidly let his guard down.

'Rather fitting you have come here, Ricky.' There stood Sydney, gun in hand, aimed at him. 'Legend says sacrifices were committed here and bodies offered to the gods. I believe a young partying couple were found here, dead, back in the day. Blood has spilt on this soil many times. In fact, I think the blood gives life to this island and keeps it fertile. Now yours will be added to it.'

Ricky raised his hands in defeat. 'OK, Sydney. You win. I am done running. I am too tired.'

Sydney smiled and walked closer. As she did this, the sun began to rise, the rain had stopped and the winds began to ease. It looked like the storm had finally passed. 'Poor old Ricky. I had you wrong about the death of my father but you were still guilty of destroying his career.'

'He destroyed his own, Sydney. Believe it or not, I felt sorry for him. I truly loved him like a brother and your mother, Mary, was a cool lady. They were well suited.'

Sydney's features softened slightly. 'Tell me about her. Do I resemble her in any way?'

Ricky had to buy himself time. Anything he said at this moment would delay the inevitable. 'In some ways, yes. Something about your eyes and some of your mannerisms.'

A small smile played on Sydney's lips. 'I have seen many photographs of her and my father of course. I had no idea for so long that my parents were world-famous. I feel cheated that I never got to meet them. Tell me more about my mother.'

Ricky pushed on. 'She was a very talented artist. She sold many of her paintings and was forging a name for herself in the contemporary art world. It was a pity about her addictions. I was truly sorry when she died.'

Ricky suddenly saw Sydney's face harden. He realised he had said the wrong thing.

'If you were so sorry maybe you should have thought about that before kicking Jimmy out of the band and then standing back and watching the man self-destruct. Obviously, it affected them both.'

Sydney aimed the gun at Ricky and he froze to the spot, waiting for the bullet to pierce his skull or heart. Sydney walked closer still, not wanting to miss her shot.

It was at that moment she unknowingly tread close to one of the island's feral cat's lairs, where she was guarding her young. The cat sprang out, spitting and snarling. It caught Sydney unaware and it distracted her momentarily. She flinched back as the cat clawed at her before disappearing back into her hole.

Ricky saw his chance and he reached down and picked up a good size rock. He felt the weight in his hand and he moved forward and smashed it down on

Sydney's head. The impact was good and Sydney collapsed to the ground. Ricky raised the rock again above his head, ready to deliver a killing blow when he heard Noah's voice shout out, 'Stop right there. Put the stone down. You better pray she is still alive otherwise your death will be slow and, I promise, painful.'

Noah was also pointing a gun at him. It was heavy-looking and black. Ricky surmised it was a Glock 17. He had handled enough mock ones in his television acting. Ricky dropped the rock.

Noah nodded. 'Looks like I got here just in time. We decided to split up to look for you. I headed over to the quayside whilst Sydney came this way to the stones. You are a slippery bastard, aren't you? Maybe you are a worthy adversary after all.'

Noah gestured with the gun and told Ricky to move away and put his back to one of the standing stones and not to move. Ricky did as he was told. 'I will have no problem putting a bullet in you but I prefer to get up close and personal, if you know what I mean,' he added. Noah pulled his coat open to reveal a wicked-looking machete in a sheath strapped across his body.

Ricky watched as Noah stooped to check on Sydney lying next to the wild cat's lair. He knew what was about to happen and he was ready to run the best he could when it did. As Noah reached for Sydney, the female cat sprang out once again and this time was able to latch on to Noah's face. He let out a yell and clawed frantically at the feline.

This was Ricky's chance. He turned and disappeared behind the stones.

Chapter 20

Ricky's heart was pounding like a steam hammer in his chest. The pain in his leg was now back with a vengeance as he hobbled as quickly as he could over the uneven terrain. He had to be careful not to slip over or trip as he knew he would now have a job to get back to his feet. The terrifying image of Noah stood over his prostrate body, ready to bring that razor-sharp machete down on his skull kept him going. He had no real idea where he was heading. He thought he might try to get to the other side of the island where Sydney had mentioned a colony of puffins were nesting. Maybe there was some sort of cave to hide out in or he might find the hidden dingy. It was a slim hope but he had nothing else to go with. He looked back over his shoulder, expecting any second to see Noah appear, but he saw nothing. Ricky hoped the cat attacking him and his concern for Sydney would keep him occupied for a little while, giving him enough time to put some distance between them.

Then into his view came one of the outbuildings that were dotted around the island. He decided to head for it. Staying in there was not an option but there might be something inside to use as a weapon.

Ricky then heard a voice shouting from a distance, 'Wilder. You are a dead man. I am coming for you.'

Ricky quickened his pace and got to the shed. He prayed the door would not be locked. Thankfully, it was open. He headed inside and drew across the bolt. It wouldn't hold long but it was some sort of protection. He looked around. It smelt of grass clippings and diesel. The shed was about ten-foot by ten-foot. It housed a couple of lawnmowers, half a dozen oil drums, a set of ladders, and various garden implements. There also were buckets, tins of paint, refuse bags, sacks and some basic tools on a battered old work bench.

He ran to the bench and scanned the tools. He picked up a chisel momentarily then decided against it. He looked again and settled on a lump hammer. Would it be a match for a machete? Who knew, but he had no choice. Ricky now looked out of the one small window in the shed. He wiped away the grime to see better and he gasped when he saw Noah a short distance away, heading towards the shed. His long trench coat flapping open in the breeze made him looking like a giant bat. Ricky could not fail to see the machete brandished in his hand. Fear flooded his body and his hands were shaking so badly that he dropped the hammer on the floor. Now that Noah was actually coming for him, he suddenly didn't feel as brave. He desperately looked around for another exit. There was none but his eyes spotted, in the corner of the shed, partially covered by an old hessian sack, a chainsaw. He took another look out the window. Noah was closer. He didn't have long.

Ricky ran to the chainsaw and picked it up. He shook it and said a silent prayer that there was diesel in it. He ripped back the cord and cursed as it didn't start. His uncontrollably shaking hands didn't help.

Noah's voice sounded outside the door. 'Little pig, little pig, let me in.' There was a loud bang on the door as Noah drove his shoulder into it. 'The big bad wolf is coming in.'

Ricky looked over his shoulder towards the door. Mercifully, for the moment, it held. He pulled the cord again. It tried to catch but no. Again, it failed. As Noah drove his shoulder into the door for a second time, the chainsaw caught and came to life just in time as the wood splintered and shattered inward. Ricky hid down by the work bench hoping to use the element of surprise to his advantage.

Noah now entered the shed. A malevolent grin spread across his face, which had been badly lacerated by the feral cat. The machete was raised above his head.

Ricky steeled himself and pushed down his fear into the pit of his belly and hobbled forward from his hiding place, slashing down with the chainsaw, ripping a huge, gaping wound in Noah's right leg. The man let out a blood-curdling scream and brought the machete downwards. Ricky managed to move backwards but the razor-sharp blade sliced the top of his right ear clean off. It was now his turn to scream out in pain.

Noah looked at the blood pouring from his leg wound. He knew it was bad but he had to finish his mission off for Sydney. Failing was not an option. He had never let her down before. Moving forward again, he swung the machete but Ricky blocked it with the chainsaw in a shower of sparks. Noah kicked him in the stomach, sending Ricky crashing back into the wall, the air driven out of his lungs. Noah saw his opportunity and walked forward, ready to administer a killing blow. 'Time to die, you bastard.'

Ricky mustered every bit of energy he had and came forward again to meet him. He then swiped the blade across Noah's midriff. The blade cut in deep and his stomach gaped open like a huge smiling mouth. His entrails spilled out of the cavity, yet, somehow, he came forward once more. Noah stopped in his tracks, looking down in surprise at the horrendous wound. Ricky swung the chainsaw once again and it bit deep into the left side of Noah's neck, instantly severing the carotid artery, spraying the shed with blood. This time, Noah fell to the ground. He lay on his back, his limbs twitching as the arterial blood spray slowed as his body bled out. Ricky dropped the chainsaw to the ground and stared down at Noah Rose, or Kenny Holton, as he'd known him, until he became still.

Shell-shocked, Ricky staggered out of the shed. He was soaked in blood, mostly Noah's. He ripped a piece of his shirt off and held it to his damaged ear. He looked up at the sky and, remarkably, a watery winter sun shone through the clouds. Slowly he headed back the way he had come, trying to process the fact he had just taken a human life in the most grotesque fashion.

Up ahead, he saw the Callanish stones. He detoured towards them and to the spot where he had hit Sydney. There was traces of blood on the ground but no body. Ricky's eyes darted everywhere, frightened that Sydney would suddenly appear and pounce on him. After a moment he relaxed. There was no sign of her. He rationalised that she had to be badly hurt and couldn't provide much of a threat to him. *Could she?* He decided his best bet was to head back to the house. Although part of him dreaded going back in there, he had try to get to a working phone or, if possible, contact Barry the boatman and tell him to come and pick him up. After all, he now knew where Mission Control was. He needed more than ever to get off this godforsaken island. He just hoped he could do this without encountering Sydney.

Chapter 21

Ricky approached the house gingerly. He scanned the windows to see if he could glimpse Sydney looking out of one of them but he saw nothing. He silently made his way up onto the porch, trying his best to avoid looking at the corpse of Brody still sat in the same position against one of the dog statues. Ricky turned the handle of the front door and it opened. Once again, he avoided the body of Erik lying face down directly in the hallway and stepped around it. It was now beginning to smell. He somehow felt numb to all the death that surrounded him.

All was quiet except for the ticking of the longcase clock. He looked towards the library door. It was wide open. He knew he had to enter it to get to Mission Control. First, though, he walked over to the other side of the hallway and picked up a wall phone and put it to his ear. He cursed under his breath as he heard no dial tone. Ricky looked back towards the library and drew in a deep breath. Adrenaline began to bubble once more in his stomach. He didn't know how much more of this he could take.

Creaking of floorboards above alerted him to the fact that somebody was upstairs. It could only be Sydney. So that meant he had a clear passage to the library. He listened again. Footsteps sounded in one of the upstairs rooms. This was his chance. He wished he could run but instead he hobbled into the library as fast as he could.

Scanning the room, he found it empty but he did notice the gun cabinet was open and there was an empty space where one of Harvey Barnes' Purdey shotguns should have been. He also saw on top of a coffee table in front of the fireplace, an open box of shotgun cartridges. The blow he had delivered to Sydney had not been, it seemed, as bad as he thought.

He moved to the study door, praying it would be open. Miraculously it was. Result. Ricky saw the two-way radio in the corner. He had used one in a boat scene whilst filming an episode of *Above the Law.* Although it had been a prop, he hoped it worked on the same principle. As he headed towards it the radio suddenly burst into life.

'Barry Skidmore calling Sydney Rose. Are you OK? Over.'

Ricky grabbed up the handset, frightened that Sydney would hear. He pressed the button to speak. 'Barry. This is Ricky Wilder from the band. Something terrible has happened over here. People are dead. I need you to phone the police and then get your boat over here as quickly as possible. Do you understand? Over.'

There was a moment of silence then Barry spoke. 'Let me speak to Sydney. Over.'

Ricky gritted his teeth and took a fleeting glance towards the door. 'Barry. I can't do that. I do not know where she is. Look, it is a long story but we haven't got time now to discuss it. This is life and death. I really need you to do what I ask. Please, Barry. Over.'

Again, a moment's silence. Then Barry spoke. 'I am on my way. I will phone the police en route. I will be as quick as I can. Over.'

Ricky said a quiet thanks to God. 'Thank you, Barry. Please hurry.'

Ricky threw down the handset. His plan now was to head down to the docking bay and wait for the boat. He moved out of the study into the library and there he saw Sydney in the doorway. The shotgun raised high. Her face was a horrific mask of dried blood. The shotgun exploded. Ricky dived back into the study as the shell smashed into the doorframe above his head, sending a shower of wood splinters everywhere. Slamming the door shut, Ricky turned the key in the lock. He frantically looked around the study for an escape route or a weapon. He saw neither. The shotgun sounded again and a hole the size of a man's fist exploded through the door.

Sydney's voice sounded. 'I underestimated you, Ricky. But I won't made the mistake a second time.'

Ricky had to find some bravado. He answered back with venom in his voice, 'Well, Noah underestimated me as well and he is now lying dead in one of the outhouses. He lost a fight with a chainsaw.'

There was a moment's silence and then the gun went off again, making the hole bigger. Sydney's face appeared at the hole. 'You bastard. You are going to die for that. You have nowhere left to go and I—.' Suddenly Sydney let out a piercing scream.

Ricky had picked up a large, pointed sliver of wood from the damaged door and drove it through the hole into Sydney's cheek. Sydney staggered away from the door, clutching at the splinter, trying to pull it free. The shotgun dropped to the floor.

Ricky turned the key in the door and came out of the study. Before Sydney could react, Ricky hit her squarely in the face with a right cross, breaking her nose. She staggered back and fell into the coffee table. Ricky reached down and picked up the shotgun. He broke it down and saw that there was still a live shell in it.

As Sydney climbed back to her feet, she reached under her coat and produced a wicked-looking hunting knife. She let out a bloodcurdling scream and rushed Ricky. For a moment, time seemed to slow down. Ricky Wilder levelled the shotgun and pulled the trigger. He watched in horrible fascination as Sydney's head exploded like an overripe melon. For a moment, her headless body carried on walking forward and Ricky recoiled in terror, but then she dropped to the floor just like a puppet that had its strings cut.

Ricky threw the gun down and collapsed exhausted onto the sofa. He held his head in his bloodstained, shaking hands and gently sobbed. The nightmare was over. Everybody was dead – slaughtered brutally in a plot that would have had Harvey Barnes salivating in anticipation of the film rights. He had no idea now what his future held without his friends and Stormtrooper but he did know he needed to finally get off the island.

It took a painful twenty minutes to reach the docking bay. Ricky sat on the edge of the quayside in a daze. Finally, he saw Barry Skidmore's boat come into view and gradually get closer and closer. When it docked, he stood up on unsteady feet and made his way towards it, relief flooding his body. The tears came again. They were uncontrollable. He saw the concerned features of Barry looking at him.

Barry Skidmore took a deep breath and for the first time ever, set foot on Ruma to help the battered figure of Ricky on board. As soon as Ricky got on the deck of the ferry, he felt things getting dark and he blacked out in Barry's arms.

Ricky recovered from his ordeal in the Glasgow Royal Infirmary. He had been airlifted to safety after Barry Skidmore had brought him back to mainland. The bullet wound in his leg had gone straight through and out the other side, no major arteries had been hit. It was healing nicely, as was his ear, and also the other cuts and abrasions he had sustained. Mentally, it was going to be some time before he would feel well. The nightmares of Ruma would probably never leave him.

The police had flooded the island after Barry had phoned them. They found what they called one of the most brutal crime scenes ever in the British Isles. Ricky had been interviewed and gave the best account he could of what had happened. He was exempt of any charges.

Over the coming weeks, they found out more on the backgrounds of Sydney and Noah Rose. Records tracked them down to their real birth parents, confirming what Sydney had told Ricky. She had been born Eve Parish-Gilmore, to birth parents, Jimmy and Mary. She was adopted by Graham and Alice Rose and renamed Sydney. Medical records had shown that Sydney had been diagnosed some years ago with bipolar disorder, which resulted in her having mood swings, bouts of anger, and violence but, somehow, she had slipped through the net, as so many do.

Noah had been born to a Thomas and Catherine. Both had died in a house fire in London. Baby Noah, who had also been in the house at the time, was saved by the emergency services and taken into care. He had been adopted at 12 months of age by Graham and Alice Rose. His army record stated that when he had left the forces, he was suffering from post-traumatic stress disorder, resulting in violent tendencies. Once out in Civvy Street, he was forgotten and swallowed up in red tape. He had been walking around like a ticking time bomb ever since. When reunited with his stepsister, they became a dangerous and potent combination. Their misplaced love and loyalty for each other resulted in the plan to kill the members of Stormtrooper in revenge for the untimely deaths of Sydney's real parents. It had been a cleverly orchestrated and devious operation which had taken some time and planning and had nearly been completely successful.

The media invaded Ruma and practically camped out there, having a field day with the story and painting lurid headlines. Harvey Barnes' quiet retreat was no longer. When Barnes had found out about the horrors that had taken place in *An Diadan*, he immediately put the house and the island on the market for sale. Whether it would sell was anybody's guess although a rumour circulated that an Arab businessman and race horse owner with more than a passing interest in the occult was keen to buy.

As Ricky got stronger, he was inundated with offers from the tabloids for his story. Every chat show host either side of the Atlantic clamoured to have him on their show. Dylan Ramsey being first in line. A new series of *Above the Law* was on the cards and Ricky could virtually name his own price. He was hot property being the only survivor of the "Ruma Isles

Slaughterhouse", as the tabloids named it. Ricky was going to be a hounded man for the foreseeable future.

Personally, it felt terribly strange for him knowing that his band mates and, of course, Bernie were no longer around. They had been on such a rollercoaster ride over the years; who would have thought it would have ended like this? Also, he felt sorrow and guilt for the others that got caught up in this madness. Brody, Jerry, Aadesh and, of course, Kerry and Jude. Some very bright lights had been tragically lost.

Ricky at present felt lost. For as long as he could remember, he had lived in a closeted world where everything was done for him. He didn't have to think for himself. Money talked and Ricky had plenty of it so he didn't have to lift a finger himself, somebody else did it. He now realised he hadn't been living in the real world for so long he had forgotten what it looked like. That was until his trip to Ruma where that had all changed. As a person, he had been stripped back to the bone and he had to resort to pure animal instinct to survive his ordeal. He was proud that he still had some sense of reality left within him to have done so. Things would be different in the future. For now, he was content to be safe and secure in the hospital and let his body heal. He would learn to take one day at a time.

Epilogue

18 months later

Ricky Wilder steps out onto the stage at London's O2 ARENA with his new band, Wilder Things. This is their second night here on a sell-out tour of the UK. Ricky, a while back, thought he would never contemplate singing or playing again but much had happened in the time since the incident on Ruma. The Stormtrooper recordings that were made on the island were found and preserved. They were remastered and the unfinished album was filled out with a few live tracks. The new and long-awaited album, now ironically named *In the Dying Light* was released in memory of the mark 2 line-up. It went instantly to number one both sides of the Atlantic and enjoyed the huge success that the band, production team and Bernie would have hoped for. It was a fitting memorial. It also drew a line under the band.

Ricky carried on with his acting and recently starred in a movie alongside Matt Damon and got rave reviews. After the success of the album, Ricky thought about finally forming a new band and killing the spectre of Stormtrooper, otherwise it would hang over him forever. Hence Wilder Things.

They had initially toured with Iron Maiden and AC/DC to see how the crowd would take to them. Ricky needn't have worried; they were warmly received and on the back of their first album release, *New Dawn,* they headlined their own tour. Ricky paid homage to Stormtrooper by playing a few of their best-known tracks but, essentially, they played their new stuff and some tracks off of Ricky's earlier solo albums.

His physical scars had healed nicely but the mental ones would take time. He had good days and bad days but he was taking it one day at a time. Six months ago, he returned to Ruma. Ironically, Barry Skidmore brought him and a small film crew over to the island to record a documentary programme for Netflix about the whole incident. Ricky had come back to lay some flowers on a memorial which had been built on Ruma in memory of those who had died there. It was a poignant and touching moment. Before going, Ricky didn't know how he would feel but he found out he was stronger than he gave himself credit for. He even walked up to *An Diadan*. At present, it was empty and the windows shuttered.

He stood in the gardens and observed it. A slight shiver ran up his spine as he recalled what had happened there. He walked up to the porch and passed the stone statues of the doors. For a moment, he visualised poor Brody sitting there, his lifeless eyes staring helplessly. Ricky shut his own eyes for a few seconds and when he opened them, the vision faded. He was glad the house was locked up; he didn't want to go inside. Walking away from *An Diadan,* he took a final glance back and thought he saw a figure looking out of one of the turret windows. Probably just a shadow or his mind playing tricks.

Ricky sailed away from the island that day with mixed emotions. Sadness but also he felt optimistic about the future. He was going to be all right.

The lights went up on stage to a huge shout from the audience as Ricky and his band opened their set with an old Stormtrooper favourite, “Tough Love”. The crowd went wild as they sung along to the iconic chorus.

Tough love is all you give me
Tough love is all I get
Tough love is all you give me
But I still want you yet.

Ricky smiled as he looked around the stage. To his left was Marshall, on his right, Rory, Erik was working his wizardly ways on the keyboards and Ray was keeping a thunderous beat on the drums. All of them a tight unit blasting out their music and then slowly they faded back to the members of Wilder Things.

As the doctors had told him, it might take a while for him to get back to some normality.

THE END

Other titles by the author published by Grosvenor House Publishing

Battlescars

Tony Slade novel number 1

Some wounds run deep. Can they ever heal?

Tony Slade sits in a coffee shop waiting. He is reflecting on his dark and violent past. He is waiting for the woman he loves, but he is also waiting for the man who wants him dead. Who will reach him first? The clock is ticking...

Tony Slade is used to dealing with violence and death. He has made a career out of it. From boxer to bouncer, paratrooper, and mercenary to minder. But now, he is getting older and he wants out. He has miraculously found love and he has one last chance at happiness, but it will come with a price. The woman he loves is not his; she belongs to a very dangerous man. A man that you don't want to cross. But Tony is ready to risk it all on one last roll of the dice before a powder keg of violence explodes.

But that is not all. Unknown to him, there is another threat coming his way. One that he will not see until the last moment. Who will get out alive?

Tough times call for tough people. Tony Slade is one such person.

No Hiding Place

You can run but you can't hide forever.

Tony Slade novel number 2

They say time is a great healer. But for Tony Slade time is running out. The physical scars are healing but the mental ones are still raw.

Waking up in hospital after the coffee shop massacre and finding he has cheated death he needs to know why?

But he has now become a man everybody wants to question.

All he wants to do is disappear forever, but some people will not let that happen.

Suddenly Tony is hounded by the press and media. He is also trailed by the tenacious DCI Wyatt and he is hunted by a psychotic killer who is relentless, and hell-bent on revenge.

Tony Slade is in hiding recovering from the bullet wounds and the trauma of recent events that have changed his life forever.

Hiding on the tiny, isolated island of *Graig O Mor* in the Bristol Channel ex-paratrooper Tony Slade knows it is only a matter of time until he is found.

Then he will have to stop running and make a stand against an enemy who will not give up. It will become a matter of life and death.

'A storm is coming from the mainland to the Island of Graig O Mor.'

Last Stand

'Blood is thicker than water'

Tony Slade novel number 3

Tony Slade is living in the Canary Islands. He is resting and soaking up the sun. He is keeping his head down under an assumed identity and trying to forget the last few traumatic years where he has experienced love, violence, heartbreak, and death.

Tony is a survivor. An ex-paratrooper and mercenary who has seen more than his fair share of action, but those days are well behind him now. Or so he thought.

He is no longer a young man and the fire that used to burn like an inferno in his belly is now just flickering. Tony is looking for a quiet life into retirement when he receives a shocking and life-changing piece of news. A secret that has been buried for years has suddenly came to light.

This secret will force Tony out of hiding to return to the UK and back into the violent world of gangsters, drugs, and crime.

Pursued all the time by an old nemesis, Tony must pull all his fighting skills together to face a dangerous and deadly drug lord who has something of his that he wants back at any cost. Tony knows that blood will spill in one final stand.

"This time, it's personal"

Killing Time

'The clock is ticking, and time is running out.'

Ex-Scotland Yard policeman, DCI Joe Regan, had retired from the force after a particularly vicious attempt on his life that had him on the critical list in hospital, but his gritty Gaelic spirit and resolve helped him recover.

Now leading a new life running an antiques emporium in the sleepy town of Oakcombe in the West Country he is trying to put his past behind him.

But unknown to Joe a burglary at the nearby country home of famous TV celebrity, Ron Goodwin, opens up a nasty can of worms in the form of something hidden within an antique clock which finds its way to his shop.

This something could ruin Ron Goodwin's career just as he is about to crack America.

The dark secrets contained within the clock cannot afford to fall into the wrong hands, so it must be found at all costs even if it means murder.

Joe Regan suddenly finds himself embroiled in a race to find the clock as it goes missing and its contents before a hired killer who will stop at nothing does.

But when Joe inadvertently stumbles across the secret, he now becomes the next target.

'The clock is ticking, and time is running out.'

A Change of Heart

'Can a heart transplant victim inherit the characteristics of their donor?'

Simon Winter is a prime candidate for a heart attack. Middle-aged, sedentary and grossly overweight. His lifestyle is driving him to an early grave but he is ignoring all the signs until it is too late.

He has a failed marriage behind him, a boring job and a fear of violence and blood. He has lived a safe and uneventful life avoiding confrontation and danger until now where this is all about to change dramatically

Eddie Prince is an ex-professional boxer and minor television celebrity. He has had a turbulent life out of the ring which has resulted in prison time. Money has come and gone as he has a gambling addiction which results in him owing a lot of money to some bad people. He has run away to what he hopes is a better life but his old life is about to catch up with him, resulting in dire circumstances.

These two men are about to connect in a way they could never have dreamed of. Two men at different ends of the spectrum. Two men who are chalk and cheese. Two men who have nothing in common until one inherits the other's heart after a transplant.

Now one will use the other as a vessel of revenge to find the man who murdered him and settle a score with shocking conclusions.

About the author

Blood Tracks is Kevin's sixth work of fiction.

His first novel was *Battlescars* (2018), where he introduced readers to the character of Tony Slade. His second novel, *No Hiding Place* (2019), continued the story. *Last Stand* (2020) gives us a trilogy of Slade adventures.

*Killing Time (*2021) then introduces the reader to a new character of Kevin's, ex-policeman turned antiques dealer, Joe Regan.

A Change Of Heart (2021) brings a different story. The intertwined lives of Simon Winter and Eddie Prince.

As well as being an author, Kevin is a globally renowned and respected martial artist. He has trained and taught for 45 years at present.

While training, he started to draft articles for martial arts magazines, which spurred him on to write a series of self-defence and combative instructional books. In 2017, he published his autobiography *When We Were Warriors*. But his real passion is to write fiction.

Kevin lives in Bristol, UK, with his wife, Tina. He is a father and grandfather.

He is now semi-retired from teaching martial arts and spends his leisure time reading, writing, playing guitar, going to the gym, and travelling.